MIRANDA'S TEMPEST

A Bribie Island Mystery

by

JULIET HOEY

MIRANDA'S TEMPEST: A BRIBIE ISLAND MYSTERY
Copyright © JULIET HOEY 2012

First published by Zeus Publications 2012
http://www.zeus-publications.com
P.O. Box 2554
Burleigh M.D.C.
QLD. 4220
Australia.

The National Library of Australia Cataloguing-in-Publication

Author: Hoey, Juliet, 1937-

Title: Miranda's tempest: a Bribie Island mystery.

ISBN: 978-1-921919-26-8 (pbk.)

Subjects: Crime--Fiction

Dewey Number: A823.4

All Rights Reserved

No part of this book may be reproduced in any form, by photocopying or by any electronic or mechanical means, including information storage or retrieval systems, without permission in writing from both the copyright owner and the publisher of this book.

This book is a work of fiction and any resemblance to any persons living or dead is purely coincidental.

The author asserts her moral rights.

© Cover Design—Bonnie Hoey 2012
Zeus Publications. Proudly printed in Australia

DEDICATION

To Denis and all the family

ACKNOWLEDGEMENTS

I would like to thank, firstly my family for their constant interest and encouragement. Special thanks must go to Denis for his invaluable plot suggestions, his meticulous proof reading and his invaluable assistance in sorting out computer problems. A big "thanks" also to my daughter-in-law Bonnie for her skill and patience in designing the cover.

My personal editor Cheryl Jorgensen once again offered excellent suggestions for improving plot structure and I am extremely grateful to her not only for these ideas but for her continuing friendliness and encouragement.

Sincere thanks to bassoonist Patricia Brennan from the Brisbane Symphony Orchestra for her very helpful information on some important but non-secret police procedures. My gratitude also goes to fellow musician, Hungarian born Greg Harty-Szabo for sharing with me the correct pronunciation of some Hungarian names. However, my character with the same surname, Szabo, is definitely not modelled on Greg!

Last but by no means least, I would like to offer heartfelt thanks to the staff of Zeus Publications, who once again demonstrated professionalism and friendly courtesy, mixed in equal doses.

***

While all characters, organisations and events in this book are entirely fictional, certain aspects of the story could not have been written without some pre-existing facts. For example, my creation of the solitary occupant of Little Goat Island, Old Seth, would have been unthinkable had I not known about the famous local identity, Mr Roy Dunlop who actually lived alone on this small island in Pumicestone Passage for many years. Like most people, I would never have believed such a lonely and dangerous existence to be possible. I stress, however, that my rather disreputable fictional character refers in no way to Mr Dunlop.

For my descriptions of rehearsals and concerts in a community orchestra, I have, naturally, drawn upon my experience as a cellist in Brisbane Symphony Orchestra. However, the Morelands Symphony is purely a figment of my imagination and if such a body actually does exist somewhere, I apologise in advance, because I have tried my best to locate it, and failed. In any case, no reference to such an organisation is intended.

Last of all, the fictional conductor of the Morelands Symphony bears no resemblance whatsoever to my friend and colleague, Antoni Bonetti, conductor of Brisbane Symphony Orchestra, for whom I have the greatest respect and admiration.

AUTHOR BIOGRAPHY

Gympie-born Juliet Hoey has lived most of her life in Brisbane. A professional musician, she graduated from the Queensland Conservatorium with a distinction in piano. She subsequently studied cello and enjoys playing that instrument in a community orchestra. With this same orchestra she has to date performed seven piano concertos. She has also given numerous solo and duo piano recitals in the course of a very busy musical career. She was an examiner in piano for many years, is a frequent adjudicator and currently teaches both piano and cello.

Writing has been a parallel passion ever since the age of nine when she found herself on holiday at Bribie Island without anything to read and solved the problem by writing a terrible book about a dog called Spotty. It sent her mother into hysterics but kept the budding author happily occupied for weeks. Three years later she won a state-wide essay competition as well as carrying off the English prize at school nearly every year. After school she majored in English at Queensland University, graduating with a Bachelor of Arts degree.

During her busy life as a musician and a mother, she still found time to write numerous articles, short stories and poetry. With her musician husband Denis, she wrote three musicals for children, one of which *The Loaded Dog,* enjoyed an immensely successful schools tour by the Queensland Opera Company. In 1986 she co-founded the national Church music magazine *One Voice* which she subsequently edited alone for five years.

In 1998 she published a non-fiction book *Under the Mulberry Tree* which describes the experience of growing up in the riverside suburb of Bulimba. Her first novel, *The Sixth Partita* was published by Zeus Publications in 2007 to critical acclaim. *Miranda's Tempest* is her second novel.

Juliet Hoey has four adult sons, an increasing number of grandchildren and a very patient husband.

PROLOGUE 5

ACT ONE 7
- *Scene One* 7
- *Scene Two* 13

ACT TWO 18
- *Scene One* 18
- *Scene Two* 23

ACT THREE 27
- *Scene One* 27
- *Scene Two* 33
- *Scene Three* 36

ACT FOUR 41
- *Scene One* 41
- *Scene Two* 49
- *Scene Three* 58
- *Scene Four* 63
- *Scene Five* 75
- *Scene Six* 77

ACT FIVE 82
- *Scene One* 82
- *Scene Two* 87
- *Scene Three* 93
- *Scene Four* 107
- *Scene Five* 111

EPILOGUE 113

She never wanted to go in the first place. For a start, she hated boats and had been terrified of water ever since that hideous day when she fell out of her brother's dinghy on the canal at the bottom of the garden. She was five years old. Visions of eerie green depths clotted with water weeds that covered her face as she struggled for breath were to haunt her for the rest of her life. She never learnt to swim.

"Don't be an old wet blanket," her husband teased, eighteen years later. "Besides, do you want to spoil our holiday?"
She hesitated, then smiled up at him. "No, I don't want to spoil it. It's all been great and tomorrow is our last day."

"Better put on plenty of suntan oil then," he returned her smile. "It's going to be a stinker of a morning."
They pushed off into the shallows of the boat ramp, and as the motor fired smartly, the little boat gained speed and made smooth headway across the clear, blue waters of the bay with only one small delay to interrupt their journey. She relaxed a little then, fears forgotten for the moment as she savoured the unfamiliar joy of cool sea winds that fanned her long, fair hair, while the gentle shoreline slipped smoothly by with languid ease as the hours passed. Nearly time to make landfall.

Morning turned to noon. Suddenly, the weather changed. Gone was the pleasant ambience of early morning. Now the sun burned down with savage cruelty from a dense bronze sky. Thick, damp air, pregnant with unshed rain, lay like a suffocating blanket upon *earth and sea, until huge black clouds appeared from nowhere to begin their mad race across the darkening sky.*

She shuffled restlessly on the hard, wooden bench, her tranquil mood gone with the coolness of the morning.

Why do I feel so frightened? It's not just the sea this time. It's not the storm that's coming, even though I can't stand storms. It's something I don't understand. It's something... *Anxious for reassurance, she looked round at him. He stood up, balancing with an easy confidence.*

"Sweetheart," he said, "I have to do this, you know. You've given me no choice."

He was smiling as he tightened the anchor rope around her neck. She was too stunned to struggle much. Yet as she sank into black depths of final nothingness in the narrow hull of the boat, she became once more the terrified child who gasped for air in the oily waters of the old canal, and with her last breath, could feel again the tangled water weeds upon her drowning face.
He sighed with satisfaction at a job well done. Cutting the motor, he eased the little boat into the shallows and brought her to shore just as the heavens opened and lightning split the purple skies. He buried her hastily beneath a pine tree while the thunder roared and swift torrents washed away her every trace from the rough wooden bench in the prow.

*

PROLOGUE

Bribie Island, Queensland

The beach at Woorim is a thousand miles from anywhere. Or so it seems. To be sure, there are signs of civilisation if you go looking for them. Behind the surf club the village clusters around its pub, its newsagent, its clutch of small, friendly shops. A mega trendy apartment block peers with funky insolence over the dunes. Nearby the lifesavers' tower performs its time-honoured task of shark-spotting and surf rescue.

All of this is attractive enough, I daresay. But it is not the Woorim that I know. It is not the beach that I adore. Instead, my small kingdom lies some distance away. Down near the end of Boyd Street just past the lookout, you come upon a small path. This sandy track ambles its way through scrubby trees and bracken to twist a little before opening out on to the beach. At the end of the path, sea and sky appear from nowhere, blue upon blue in a frame of dark green. The magic never fails. Through this enchanted portal I am gently led into another world, a *Narnia* of my own making.

From my vantage point under the shade of the casuarina trees I can look out now across the boat passage to Moreton Island. Swathed in its gauzy scarf, the ever-changing colours mirror the caprices of the weather – today pale blue, tomorrow soft amethyst. Sometimes, darkly menacing, it turns into a monster of jagged, grey hills which sulk beneath angry clouds. At other times the distant island retreats behind a curtain of fine, misty rain to disappear from view altogether. How easy then to imagine that there is no Moreton at all, that Bribie exists alone in these wild waters, a castaway's refuge adrift in an endless sea.

*

This is Miranda's story, not mine. I suppose I should let her tell it herself. Indeed I begged her to, but she was adamant right from the beginning.

"You tell it, Veronica," she insisted. "You're the one with the gift of the gab. And you were involved right from the word 'go'. I'd only get it all muddled. Besides, I still find it hard sometimes even to think about it."

I could well understand that. Still, I hesitated.

"Please!" she continued, "you're the one who helped me most, the whole way through and especially at the end. You and Sarah. The way you both worked it all out was just brilliant. If you hadn't, they wouldn't have got to me in time. I'd have died on the spot. You know that."

I sighed. "Okay. You win. But what about all those occasions when I wasn't there with you? You'd have to fill me in on them. And do you really think you could face having to go over the whole thing again, and then telling me exactly how it happened?"

She nodded. "I know I'll find it hard, but it's such an unbelievable story, it has to be told," she replied firmly, "and you're the only person I can trust to tell it."

ACT ONE

Bribie Island, September 2004

"Come unto these yellow sands,
And then take hands."
(Shakespeare: *The Tempest,* Act One, Scene One)

Scene One

I got up reluctantly from my sandy perch under the dunes. Time to get back to the cottage. I had been here on the beach for well over an hour and the others would be sending out a search party if I didn't turn up soon. One of the penalties of ageing. It never ceases to amuse me. Behold me, a fit, healthy specimen in my seventies, more than capable of looking after myself. I watch what I eat. I take care of my health. I exercise six days a week. I am quite street-smart. Yet none of this ever stops my daughter Helen, my son-in-law Andrew and yes, even my darling grandchildren from imagining that I'm in constant danger of being attacked by gangs of bogans roaming the dunes with razor-sharp knives, or at the very least, of being torn to shreds in the jaws of designated man-eating sharks with my name engraved on their fins.

I walked the short block back to the house and started rinsing the sand off my feet at the outside tap.

"Nanny, you've been gone simply ages. Mum was just going up to see if you were alright." James is eleven years old, and responsible for the world.

"It's okay, sweetie. You know what I'm like once I get anywhere near water ... Damn! I've got jellyfish bites all over my ankle."

"Serves you right, you old gadabout," reproved Helen, coming out on to the veranda and brandishing a salad server. "Anyway, you're back just in time. Andrew's taken the other two over to Bongaree to get the fish for tea. They'll be back any minute."

"In that case, I'm disappearing into the shower before Bedlam sets in."

"Too late! Bedlam has arrived," announced Andrew from behind an enormous white packet. "Hurry up, Jonathan ... Clare, do you think that you could manage to walk a straight line instead of cart-wheeling across the floor?"

"Oh Dad! I have to keep practising my routines every spare second. My grading's next week and..."

"For pity's sake, the lot of you, will you come and sit down before it all gets stone cold."

*

We spend as much time up here as we can. I am supposed to be retired. Somehow I can't see it's ever happening. Musicians seldom retire, they just do less. I am past retiring age, but still have a sizeable music teaching practice in Brisbane. My house at McDowall is well set up with its studio – well, actually, with its two upstairs studios, because Helen also taught from home before she married. When she left, I had the wall between the two rooms knocked out to make one large area, ideal for student concerts. I also accompany quite a bit, and still do some examining.

"You'll kill yourself," proclaims Sarah. Dear Sarah. Dramatic, generous, impulsive, eternally shrouded in Celtic gloom, my old maid elder sister has spent a lifetime worrying over me. At the age of nearly eighty she's not about to change, either.

"It's the Hogan coming out in you," I tease her.

Helen is my only child. James and I married fairly late, and we were lucky to manage even one baby. We treasured every minute that we had, perhaps sensing that our time together would be all too short, as indeed it was. One unforgettable night it was all over. Helen was only twenty and right in the middle of her music degree course at the Queensland Conservatorium. I was jolted awake by my husband's pathetic struggle to breathe. Frantically, I tried CPR while screaming at Helen to call an ambulance. It was no good. James Henry O'Donnell, medical practitioner, aged fifty-six, was pronounced dead on arrival at Royal Brisbane Hospital.

We shared a few sad years, just the two of us then, our sorrow made even deeper by the dreadful thing that happened to Helen three years later in London. She was spending a few months studying the keyboard music of Bach with an acclaimed Baroque specialist. We nearly lost her there one cold spring night, when she clung to life by a thread, alone and in an alien land.

How often we look at her now, Andrew and I, with a silent prayer of thanks for a precious life so nearly lost.

*

"Mum," asked Jonathan through a mouthful of cod, "is Miranda coming tomorrow?"

Miranda Thomas went through the Conservatorium with Helen and has been like one of the family ever since.

Helen and I exchanged glances.

"I don't know, love. She said she'd like to, but she has a lot of theory papers to mark ... I'm sure she'll come if she can."

'That's good," chimed in Clare. "She promised to play some duets with me. She's *such* a cool sight reader. She can play anything you whack in front of her. Awesome."

"I know," groaned Helen. "She makes me sick."

Helen's sight-reading has always been the weak link in her musical armoury. I should know. I taught her right up until her Con audition.

"Well anyway," James waved his fork in the air, "at least Patrick and Fabian might come too. I'm dying to go to the pool with them."

"Don't get your hopes up, mate," replied Andrew kindly. "I don't know if Michael is free to bring their boys up. It might be just Miranda on her own, or it might even be nobody at all. In which case you'll just have to put up with this boring old Carlisle family for the rest of the week."

"Well, one can always live in hope," intoned James. James's nose is permanently glued to a book. He collects quotations the way other kids collect bugs.

*

"What gives with Miranda and Michael now?" asked Andrew. The children were all in bed, hopefully out of earshot.

"Last I heard she thought she might give him another chance. Mind you, she's terribly cut up. I don't think she really knows what she wants at this stage."

"Did you actually ask her?"

"Yes I did. But it was only a five-second conversation behind a pillar at the last examiners' meeting," replied Helen. "Besides, walls have ears."

"Especially musos. That's why some of them have perfect pitch. To catch all the gossip."

"Anyway, I'm not all that hopeful. She's just so hurt I really don't know if she could ever manage to forgive him. I'm not sure if I could, either, in her shoes."

"He's an idiot," scowled Andrew. "Doesn't know a good thing when he's on to it."

"How did it all start?" I asked.

Helen looked thoughtful. "Apparently at a music camp." She took another sip of her coffee. "Well, you know how it is. You work your butt off all day conducting and tutoring stacks of kids. You put up with the excruciating noises they make if they're only string beginners, or with indifferent singing if it's choirs you're doing. After a hundred years, you get them all to bed. Then some poor suckers have to stay on up duty parading outside the cabins until the last brat subsides into slumber while the rest of the staff go off and have drinkies in their quarters. Anyway, this particular night, Michael and this bird drew the short straw of night patrol. I hear she's a bit of a slag. They got talking, she gave him the come on, one thing led to another and a few nights later, hey presto, a romantic tryst down behind the sand dunes."

"No!"

"Oh yes!"

"How did Miranda find out?" I asked.

"Well, he told her. As soon as he got home, she knew there was something wrong and eventually managed to worm it out of him."

"At least that's better than hearing it from some gossip or other."

"I suppose it does indicate an apelike kind of conscience, buried a long way down... If only I could get my hands on him..."

"Just what would you do, sweetheart?" Andrew suppressed a grin.

"Oh it's funny, is it?"

"Of course it's not funny. It's bloody awful. I'm just trying to picture little old you trying to bash up someone Michael's size." Helen smiled in spite of herself.

"Anyway," I put in, "Michael's always liked his bit of skirt, hasn't he? Remember the way he used to drool over Diane Forsayth's cleavage all those years ago, even though he couldn't stand her as a person?"

Andrew agreed. "With Michael, it was all about sex. I thought he'd grown up a bit since then, but you never know how people are going to break out."

"You know, he really does adore Miranda," I said thoughtfully.

"Yes, and he has a great way of showing it, hasn't he?" Helen was in tears.

I put my arm around her. "They'll sort it out, love. Just give them time."

Andrew reached over the table to hold her hand. "You know, it was probably just a one off thing," he said. "I mean, one of those stupid flings done in a rare moment of weakness. I'm sure he's really sorry now... Of course, I know that's no excuse."

"Well, anyway," Helen wiped her eyes, "I suppose all we can do is to give poor old Miranda lots of TLC. And then just wait and see."

"Meanwhile trying to be civil to Michael," warned Andrew.

"Now that," replied Helen, "may be rather difficult."

Miranda did come the next day. Without Michael or the boys.

"I just need to get away from the lot of them," she shrugged. "I simply can't do the happy family act at the moment. And anyway, the twins always like having their father to themselves for a while."

"Come on, Mrs Healy. Get your togs on and come down to the beach," Helen coaxed, giving her a big hug. "The sea's wonderful therapy, you know. And it will help take your mind off things for a while."

Scene Two

Bribie Island

There's something spooky about water. Source of life and giver of pleasure, this precious gift is a two-edged sword. Sustainer and destroyer, enabler and killer, it both fascinates and repels. It has done this to the human race since the dawn of creation when "the Spirit hovered over the waters".

I have always loved the water. As a land-locked child in Ipswich I would run down to the river whenever I could, spending hours beside the muddy Bremer, my toes in the shallows, idly dreaming through the green and gold of a late summer's day. Or in the holidays at nearby College's Crossing on the Brisbane River where our parents sometimes took us for picnics and for swims, the drowsy afternoons seemed swathed in a timeless ambience which went on forever until day melted into night and bright starlight illumined our journey home.

Likewise, the sea was a big part of my childhood. I first came to Bribie when I was eight, my sister eleven. What an adventure! No bridge then. You came to the island by boat. After the long trip down the river and across the bay from Redcliffe, arrival at the Koopa jetty always seemed to the intrepid travellers as exciting as the arrival of Marco Polo after his epic journeys. Neither was there any electricity on the island for those first few visits. How well I can remember my mother muttering discreet swear words as she battled each day with an unfamiliar wood stove and kerosene lamps, both of which drove her to distraction. As for Sarah and myself, we simply adored it. To go to bed using only lamps or candles was the epitome of romance, never mind the ever-present risk of setting ourselves on fire. And over it all, forever shielding this enchanted kingdom, the pervading scent of wood smoke and island pine trees mingled with sea air to create an aroma of pure magic, a fragrance long since gone, but to me the very soul of Bribie.

When Helen was only little, James and I bought our holiday cottage, not on the passage side but at Woorim, a stone's throw from the ocean beach. We used it as often as we could, allowing for my husband's murderously busy workload. Like all suburban doctors at that time, James was consistently overworked, and indeed, were it not for his terrible workload, I might still have had him today.

One evening many years ago, with young Helen safely tucked up in bed under the watchful eye of her Aunt Sarah, my beloved and I had strolled down to the beach for a rare romantic moment together. We stood for quite a while, arm in arm on top of the dunes. For once, we had the place all to ourselves. But as we gazed into the peaceful darkness, this queer thing happened. It happened to both of us, and it happened so unexpectedly that we almost gasped for breath. For no apparent reason, we were enveloped in a silent terror as the scene appeared to change before our incredulous eyes. Suddenly the sea transformed itself from the benign companion of our sunlit days into a hideous monster, a thing of menace, its heaving waters black with hidden secrets of evil and untold horror. The feeling was raw, elemental, terrifying. Clutching hands, we turned tail and ran the whole way back to the cottage.

Afterwards, neither of us could ever explain this curious experience. Had I been alone, I might well have put the whole thing down to an overheated imagination, but we had both felt it. We had both been frightened beyond rational cause. I have since come to believe that we had been touched by something so pagan and so primitive that it was like a veil parting before our sophisticated twentieth-century eyes. For a brief instant, these gossamer threads had blown aside to reveal the astonishing scene before us. Privileged or otherwise, we had been transported into a world before time – a world without heart, without mercy, without the softening touch of intelligent life. I still shudder at the memory.

*

On the last day of the September holidays, I drove up to White Patch. Miranda had gone back to Brisbane. The others wanted to come with me, but the kids were engrossed in a game of Monopoly and Helen and Andrew were enjoying a brief hour of quiet reading before the onslaught of lunch. I had no wish to disturb this rare moment of peace.

"Besides," as I said to Helen, "much as I love you all to bits, I do like my own company too... It's okay, Andrew, *don't fuss!* I've got my mobile. I'll be back in time for lunch. See ya!"

White Patch is one of my favourite parts of the island. Just outside the National Park, it is surrounded by bush, wild and beautiful, a memorial to the Bribie of my childhood when civilisation was still a few years away. Nobody ever goes there except the handful of residents who live along the esplanade and the occasional fisherman or picnicker. Today I had the place all to myself. Or I thought I did. Sitting on the wooden steps that lead down to the beach, I was suddenly disturbed by a cough. I looked up. Old Seth was walking along the shore with his dog, a mangy mutt of uncertain lineage with one brown ear, one black ear and a body all shades in between.

Seth was a colourful local character with a wealth of yarns to spin. I had come across him from time to time over the years. He lived alone on one of the many uninhabited islands in Pumicestone Passage. North of Gallagher Point and just off mainland Donnybrook, Little Goat Island is scarcely tourist-brochure material. Surrounded largely by mangrove swamps, it nevertheless contains enough firm ground to support a small shack and enough soil to grow a few vegetables and fruit trees. Presumably these are what keep Seth from starvation, these and whatever fish or crabs he can manage to catch either from his tinny or from the rickety jetty to which the tinny is usually tethered. Every so often, he emerges from his self-imposed exile to putter south in his small craft if he needs something from the Big Smoke. Last time he had come to Brisbane was four years ago when a brief illness forced him into Prince Charles Hospital for a week and much to his disgust, they cut his hair.

"Hello, Seth," I called out.

He looked up and grunted a reply, "No yabbies here. Might as well 'ave stayed home. Coulda saved a bit of fuel."

"Rough on the water today?"

"Nah! Takes more wind than this to scare me orf."

He continued to poke around on the sand for a few minutes longer, no doubt searching for the non-existent yabbies while the mutt mooched over to a dead tree branch looking for a place to wee.

Finally abandoning his search, Seth came up, leaned his wizened frame against the stair rail and rolled a fag with tobacco out of a tin that must have predated World War II. I wondered when he had last had a bath and tried very hard to breathe through my ears.

"Gawd, but there's some idiots out on the water."

"Oh?"

"Yesterdey I was doin' some fishin' just off Banksia Beach and what do I see? This big, flash cabin cruiser about four mile long sailin' way too close to that old wreck."

"You mean the *Avon*?"

"Yair, that's it. Anyway, they was that close they practically shaved the top orf the deck with their hull. You could actually see all them old bits of rust stickin' up outta the water beside the cruiser. Must have been blind. Or pissed... Bloody morons."

"What did you do?"

"Me? Yelled out to 'em, of course. Then this character in his designer hat and sunnies just turns around as if he has all day, gives me the royal wave and keeps goin'. Missed the wreck by inches."

"Crikey!"

Seth took a disgusted drag on his weed. The dog, having finished his essential business, loped over to the steps and nuzzled a black snout up against his owner's leg.

"I wonder just how many other wrecks are half buried in the passage?" I mused.

"Dunno about that. But I can tell yer this much, lady. There's more things down there in Davy Jones' locker than yer could poke a stick at. Struth, but I've seen some strange sights in me time."

"Like what?"

"Tide's turnin'. Gotta go. Take all day to tell yer. Maybe next time... Come on, Buster. Into the yacht."

"See you, Seth."

He ambled off to his decrepit old tinny. But I sat there for a long time, staring out to sea. I couldn't get his words out of my mind. Like an unpleasant fragment of a melody that wouldn't go away, they continued to haunt me, a chorus to tease the imagination. *'There's more things down there in Davy Jones' locker than yer could poke a stick at.'*

What did you mean, Seth? What things are down there? Just harmless old wrecks like the *Avon*? Or is there something more? I thought of sailors lost at sea, of travellers washed overboard, of bones washed clean by endless tides. I thought of ancient wrecks, their rotting timbers hiding ghastly secrets fathoms deep in ocean vaults. I pondered tales of ghost ships like the *Marie Celeste* with its spectral hulk forever doomed to float in eerie silence upon an empty sea. I remembered the night-ocean and the terrors of a summer's evening with my husband by the shore. But James was long since gone, and there was no one now to share my fear.

I felt a sudden chill. Time to go back.

ACT TWO

Brisbane

"Foot it featly here and there,
And, sweet sprites, the burden bear."
(*The Tempest,* Act One, Scene Two)

Scene One

"So you're back from Prospero's island?"
"Pardon?"
"Miranda, my dear. Don't tell me you've never read *The Tempest*?"
"No. Should I?"
"With a name like yours, yes, you should."
"Why that play in particular?"
John Abbott leaned back against the doorframe, looking as if he had just discovered a new continent. The sight of that smug expression on his face always made Miranda itch to box his ears.
"Well, you see, Miranda is the heroine in *The Tempest* and Prospero was her father. And when Miranda was only a small child, there was a storm at sea and they were both shipwrecked on this island where they lived as castaways for many years. Prospero's island. That's where the play was set. You simply must read it before you're much older."
"Then I guess I'll have to, won't I? In my abundant spare time. And yes, I am back from the island, as you can see, and no, I'm

afraid it's not Prospero's island even though my name is Miranda. It's only Bribie Island."

"Quite so. I first visited Bribie briefly when I was up here on holidays once, but I'm afraid..."

Miranda sneaked a look at her watch.

"John, I'm very sorry. I don't want to seem rude, but we really must start David's lesson. I have a pretty tight schedule this afternoon and I can't afford to run late. You know how it is."

"So sorry, my dear. You know I always enjoy our little conversations. I'll be back in half an hour to collect my young man. On the dot. Promise."

"Come along, David. Let's have a look at your practice record for this week."

*

Miranda was in no mood to suffer John Abbott and his pompous twitterings.

Or the spasmodic laziness of young David. On the whole, she quite liked John. It was just that at the moment, everything seemed to irritate her. After all, it was only four weeks after Michael's betrayal and she was barely hanging together. The raw wounds smarted afresh each time she thought about the whole wretched thing – though heaven knows, she tried with all her being to avoid thinking about it. The very idea of her adored husband with another woman made her feel physically ill.

Work was a lifesaver. Miranda had a large music teaching practice. She was an excellent teacher with a well-deserved reputation as one of the best piano teachers in Brisbane. Unlike my Helen who would always need the musical outlet of performing as well as teaching, Miranda was totally fulfilled by the nurturing of talent in others. In teaching, she had found her niche. Michael was equally content in his work, though in the very different field of class music. As a bonus, their hours as teachers dovetailed perfectly with the needs of their little boys, Patrick and Fabian.

Michael was a good father, and a supportive, helpful husband – at least until now.

During small breaks in the course of the long afternoon, Miranda found her thoughts straying to John Abbott, probably because anything that blotted out Michael was a welcome distraction.

Abbott was a new addition to the local music scene. Trained at the Royal College of Music in London, he had come to Australia as a young man to lecture in piano at the Sydney Conservatorium. After a successful career performing and teaching piano, as well as branching out into conducting, he had retired to Brisbane, presumably preferring the slightly slower pace of the sleepy sub-tropical city.

"I was sick of the rat race, Miranda," he would say. "Besides which, in any big institution you've always got to watch your back. I'm quite happy to be shot of it all. Anyway, Marjorie and David both adore Brisbane."

Abbott's reasons for choosing Brisbane seemed plausible enough. Yet before very long, a few cynics began to suspect that despite his undoubted skills, the splash made in the crowded Sydney pond during his long career there had probably not been quite big enough to satisfy the inflated ego of this particular frog. Now in semi-retirement, the Brisbane puddle offered the promise of bigger waves with fewer swimmers getting in the way.

It didn't surprise anybody, then, when the new arrival wasted no time in starting a music studio, joining the Music Teachers' Guild and, in rapid succession, getting himself elected firstly on to the council and finally ending up as president. At the same time, he approached various community orchestras seeking engagements as guest conductor. On the whole, people found John Abbott pleasant, charming, capable and interesting. He was mostly well liked. And certainly, all of this activity was harmless enough. What was sometimes irritating to the discerning few was the air of amused condescension that accompanied it.

Miranda had just finished the last lesson when there was a knock at the door. She had been desperate for a loo break and a cup of coffee for the last hour. Damn!

"Oh, hello, John. What brings you back?"

"So sorry to intrude, my dear. I was just in the next street on my way to the garage when I remembered something I had to ask you."

Miranda suppressed a sigh. "You'd better come in for a minute, then."

Abbott stretched his long legs in front of the armchair. It was clear that he had time to spare.

"What gives, John?"

"A little matter I neglected to raise with you. I've just been asked to guest conduct the next concert for the Morelands Symphony Orchestra."

"That's great!"

"Yes, rather! Their committee has picked some good stuff this time. We're doing Liszt's *Les Préludes*, Kodály's *Dances of Galanta* and *Háry János*."

Miranda looked puzzled.

"Nice program. But where do I come in?"

"Aha! I knew you'd ask that. Well, here it is. Did you know that the *Háry János* has two keyboard parts, one for piano and one for cimbalom?"

"No, I didn't. I'm afraid I've only heard it once or twice."

"Then you're in for a pleasant surprise, and not just because it's a great piece, either."

"Go on."

"How would you like to do one of those parts?"

How would she! Miranda had never done any orchestral keyboard playing but had always wanted to. At times, she had even envied Andrew with his job as a professional cellist and Helen, who had done so well with cello as second instrument at the Con that she was now a regular player in the Morelands Symphony.

"I'd love to, John. But why not Helen? She'll be in the concert, anyway, won't she? She'd be right on the spot."

"Yes, I certainly did think of Helen as an obvious choice, but you see, she really can't be spared from the cellos. We're down two players in the section, anyway."

"Well, what about Veronica, then? She's still doing quite a bit of playing and I know she'd do a really good job"

"I've already asked her. She's quite keen to do it. But remember, there are two keyboard parts. One for her, and one for you."

"Wow! So there are... Okay, John, then I'll say yes. As long as the dates suit and I have enough time to practise."

"That's settled, then. You won't be sorry. It's a super piece."

"I know. I'll look forward to it. And thanks for asking me, John."

At least it will take my mind off Michael for a bit longer, she thought. And what fun it will be to work with Veronica and Helen in the same concert!

Scene Two

Brisbane and Bribie

It was a sunny morning in October. Helen and I were sharing a precious moment together in a coffee shop at Flockton Village. Only last year we had decided that despite the usual family comings and goings, we really weren't seeing enough of each other. We found we were both missing the one-to-one sharing we had always enjoyed so much.

Normally we kept our socialising to about an hour, but today was different. For once, we had the luxury of an entirely free morning. It was a pupil-free day, and most of our younger students found the company of their friends a tad more alluring than the inside of a music studio.

"I think I'll have to buy a chest of drawers for the cottage," I announced, lounging back after our second flat white.

"What on earth for? That place is bulging at the seams already."

"I know it is. But there never seems to be enough storage space. You know how it is. The kids go up there and even if it's only for a weekend, there's mess everywhere. Clothes, books, toys, beach balls, boogie boards, stuff all over the floor ... yes, you know what I'm going to say, don't you? It jars my slats."

Helen laughed.

"Well, blame their father. Andrew Carlisle is the untidiest human being God ever put breath into. The kids must get it from him."

"Pathetic, isn't it? Anyway, I thought a chest of drawers might just do the trick. They can stick all their revolting gear in there out of sight and then I won't be risking a stroke."

Helen looked thoughtful.

"Tell you what, Mother dear. Why don't we go to over to Thompson's Treasure House and see what they've got?"

"What! Now?"

"Well, why not? We're both free agents for a few hours, Andrew's home this morning with the kids and heaven knows we don't often get a chance like this."

"Are you sure you can spare the time? ... Okay then, let's go."

*

Apart from our relaxing coffee meetings, the month of October was proving its usual frantic round of exam preparation, students' concerts, catching up of missed lessons, and in between all this madness, trying to do enough practice myself to keep on top of things. The end of the year is a nightmare for musicians. The debilitating heat doesn't help, either. However, this time I was lucky. By some astute juggling, I achieved the rare luxury of all four weekends at the beach. It saved my sanity.

The family came with me on the very last weekend. For a wonder, there were no orchestral concerts for Andrew, no school speech nights for the kids, no exams for any of our students. I must confess that this time my hospitality had an ulterior motive. I needed the loan of Andrew's trailer to get the newly bought chest of drawers up to the cottage.

"Ye gods, Veronica, how old is this crate?" gasped Andrew, red-faced with exertion. "It weighs a ton, too."

"Sorry, old friend. It was love at first sight."

"Well, I hope your love is reciprocated. It's going to be a lot of work, you know."

I did know. But then I have always loved beautiful things. I never tire of restoring them. The whole process of stripping old polish, sanding, varnishing, and examining the finished product fascinates me. Anyway I believe that many things improve with age. Including people.

"Mum," Helen broke into my reverie, "look what I've found!"

"What?"

"Here. In this drawer. Second one down."

Trying not to sneeze, I stuck my head into its cavernous mustiness and gingerly pulled out a fragile page of old newspaper lining.

"What's so special about this?"

"Just read it."

AAP Reuter. Vienna.

Authorities are searching for a suspect wanted for the murder of music student Heinrich Schwartzkopf whose body was retrieved from the Salzach River, Salzburg, in the early hours of August 13th. After an apparently unprovoked struggle on the riverbank, the suspect was observed running from the scene of the crime, but disappeared as the witness gave chase.

The witness, Hans Köller, was able to identify the attacker as a Hungarian expatriate, Ferenc Johannes Szabo, fellow student of the Mozarteum. A major music competition was scheduled for the following week and it is suggested that professional jealousy could have been a possible motive for this apparently unprovoked attack. It is feared that the suspect may have somehow succeeded in leaving the country, as so far he has continued to elude detection.

The Courier-Mail. August 20th 1956

"Gosh! I wonder if they ever found him"

"He might have gone AWOL. You know, like that train robber, Ronnie Briggs. Look how he managed to hole up in Brazil for all those years."

"That's right, Andrew. He could be anywhere."

"Professional jealousy does awful things, doesn't it?" said Helen.

"Sure does," I agreed. "I read a lot of detective stories and..."

A loud groan from Helen.

"Alright, alright. I agree. It's almost an addiction."

"It IS an addiction. Anything to do with crime. You know, Andrew, if she ever has to miss an episode of *The Bill,* she breaks out in a huge, red rash."

"Alright, miss. Enough out of you. I was GOING to say that it's amazing the motives behind murder."

"Ambition. Revenge. Sexual jealousy. Greed. Fear. What a list." Andrew ticked them off on his fingers.

"And perversion," muttered Helen.

Dangerous ground here.

"Anyway, this character is probably dead by now." I swiftly changed tack.

"Nanny, have you finished looking at that old wardrobe thing yet? We're all STARVING." Jonathon was standing dejectedly in the doorway, doing a pretty good imitation of Oliver Twist on workhouse rations.

Cursing my creaking knees, I got to my feet.

"Okay, love. Sorry we took so long. We're finished for now. Chow time."

ACT THREE

Brisbane

"A solemn air,
And the best comforter."
                              (*The Tempest*, Act Five)

Scene One

The rehearsals for the final concert season of the Morelands Symphony Orchestra were well under way, with two evenings already having been scheduled for the *Háry János Suite*. Helen and I were driving home along Kedron Park Road, dissecting the rehearsal and enjoying the usual orchestra gossip.

"What do you think of Abbott's conducting, Mum?" asked Helen as we swung around the corner past the Kedron Park Hotel and out into Gympie Road.

"Well, he certainly knows what he's doing. I do think he yaks a bit too much though. Wastes a lot of time trying to be funny."

"Oh, we all know that. You get used to it after a while. By the way, how do you think Miranda's managing?"

"She's great. I was pleasantly surprised because she always runs her own playing down so much."

"I know. She was like that at the Con. You could never convince her that she was any good."

"What a shame! By the way, who's that weird guy at the back of the first violins? He wears little round glasses and has bad hair."

Helen laughed.

"That could only be our dear friend Frank. Frank Sardor. Why do you ask?"

"Well, he was giving Miranda the once over every time I looked at him. Seemed to be practically undressing her with his frog's eyes. Gave me the creeps."

Helen grimaced. "Ugh! Yucksville Incorporated. Thinks he's God's gift to women because he's cultured and European. Not like us rough colonials."

"European? Where does he come from?"

"Not sure. One of those central European Eastern Bloc countries. Could be Hungary or Romania or somewhere. Wish he'd go back to where he came from."

"What's his story?"

"Well, he hasn't been playing with us for very long but I do know this much. He's just retired from the State Orchestra. Andrew came across him there at work but of course didn't have much to do with him, being in a different section. He's a thorough pain in the proverbial."

It was my turn to laugh. "Why in particular? Apart from having bad hair and the wrong kind of glasses?"

"It's because he's been a professional violinist," Helen replied disgustedly, "so you see, naturally he thinks he's God's gift to a mere community orchestra like ours and absolutely HATES being put at the back of the section. He sulks for the first half of every rehearsal."

"And just why is he back there if he's been a pro?"

"Because our concertmaster Janet makes all newcomers sit at the back for the first season, no matter how good they are. It's really much fairer to the long-standing players and also it nips any ego problems in the bud before they even start."

"Good idea."

"Yes, I think so too. Furthermore, most of our string sections change their seating plan for each concert. We think this works well; it's so much fairer and keeps us all on our toes, having to play from different positions in the section. Anyway, this dear boy is mortally insulted at being put at the back. And I reckon he won't be satisfied until he's worked his way up to concertmaster."

"How childish."

"I couldn't agree more. I mean, it's a community orchestra, for heaven's sake, and a good one too. But it's hardly the Berlin Phil."

"Then Janet had better watch out," I chuckled.

We pulled up outside my house in Walpole Street. Instantly the porch light went on.

"Aunt Sarah," Helen giggled, "your personal bodyguard."

"Still has to look after the little sister." I smiled.

"Mum, it's only because she cares. And it makes Andrew and me feel so much better knowing that there are two of you in that house."

"I know. And thank God for that, too... Well, night night, love. Thanks for the lift."

I turned and went inside under the watchful gaze of two affectionate pairs of eyes. Satisfied of her mother's safety, Helen reversed the car ready for the short drive home to Mitchelton.

London – 1957

He should never have come to England. But then, it really wasn't his choice. Like so many other unpleasant decisions in his short life, this last, most radical one had been forced upon him by circumstances quite beyond his control. Or so he believed.

It all started in his native land. Hungary, 1955 – a living nightmare from which he had made a miraculous escape, arriving in Salzburg with nothing but a few miserable forints in his wallet and a single change of clothes. Austria, that safe haven in a world torn apart by political madness, was a place in which he could finally begin the slow, agonising task of rebuilding a shattered life.

At first he did very well. His German was good. He was prepared to try anything, he was not afraid of hard work. Six months of grinding, twelve-hour days washing dishes and waiting on tables in a grungy little café down a dirty side street earned him just enough money to scrape together a deposit on a student level violin. But that was only the beginning. For a further six months, each night he drove his exhausted body and mind through the barriers of a fatigue that literally made him sick as he stood in his dingy little room practising for two solid hours. His boss told him it was sheer madness, and indeed it was. But again, what choice did he have? How else could he possibly hope to rebuild a technique ruined, like every other damned thing he had ever cared about, by the upheavals of the last two years?

It was all so unfair. Life was unfair. But eventually his luck did turn. His musical education in Hungary had been excellent, his basic string technique solid and reliable. So after the gruelling months of intensive practice, he finally took his courage in his hands and auditioned for a place at the Mozarteum. To his great delight, he was accepted into the course.

*

It would have been alright if only they hadn't found out. The teaching staff. Too ready to listen to all the silly rumours, too quick to condemn on mere hearsay. Yes, he was overly competitive, yes there had been some scuffles with other students, and yes, there had been the occasional disagreements that had degenerated into shouting matches with a few punches thrown in the heat of the moment. But surely this was nothing serious, nothing more than mere student high spirits? Trust the hierarchy to blow it all out of proportion. They even accused him of being violent. Violent? What an injustice! Of course he wasn't violent. How could they say that? He was just looking after himself in a rough world.

It got much worse. Gradually this generalised disapproval filtered down from staff to students, and soon even his friendliest classmates were beginning to shun him; to exclude him from not only their social life, but sometimes even from their conversations. His pride could not bear such treatment. He was making plans to leave, but one final, disastrous, contretemps was to make the leaving urgent.

*

"You don't need to do that any more, Sardor," his companion joked as they walked together up Exhibition Road on their way to the Royal College of Music. "You're not in Hungary now, you know, or even in Austria. The way you look over your shoulder all the time gives me the creeps. You'd think that the Secret Police were hiding in every doorway. Why do you keep on doing it? You're safe in this country."

Why? He didn't know why. He knew only that after a lifetime of such tortured vigilance, the habit was still unshakeable. Besides, there was that other matter, the one he never intended to happen, the one that nobody in England knew about. And you could never be sure just who you could trust, especially here, in this strange, hostile land a world away from anything he had ever known in Europe.

At first he found the English language surprisingly difficult, but as his mastery improved, he became quite a good student academically and a more than average violinist with a secure technique that could possibly get him into a professional orchestra upon graduation if he worked hard enough and got all the breaks. But he was no virtuoso. In his heart, he knew this. Which is why he detested that upstart pianist, that insufferable John Abbott with his film star looks that sent all the female students into paroxysms of suppressed lust. It wasn't fair!

This alone would have been bad enough. But there was more. As well as charming the pants off half the student population, the detestable creature had managed to wrap the entire teaching staff around his little finger, too. The way they all raved about his outstanding abilities and predicted a bright future for their golden haired boy made the plodding, unattractive Hungarian seethe with impotent rage.
"It's just because he knows how to slime his way around the right people," Sardor would fume to himself. "One day I'm going to kill the bastard."

*

Scene Two

Brisbane

I don't know just when I started to feel really worried about Miranda. At first the feeling was so vague that I was barely even aware of it. Naturally we, her dearest friends, had been concerned for her ever since we heard about Michael's little roll in the hay. We had tried as unobtrusively as possible to offer whatever support we could. We had invited her up to the cottage whenever it could be arranged – all the usual sorts of things that decent people do for friends in need.

However, something was different now. From this seed of normal compassion there began to sprout a plant more sinister, a tangled weed of noxious anxiety to invade my consciousness, often when I least expected it. At first it was just the little things, those tiny, insignificant clues barely noticed but stored in the memory for some future reference. Like Miranda's lovely hair, dark and fluffy but always neat, now sometimes looking as if it hadn't seen a brush in days. Or the carelessly matched colours on a girl so often admired for her meticulous dress sense. Or occasionally a sharp word in reply to a perfectly innocuous remark which would startle the listener. This was not the Miranda we all knew and loved. Something was very wrong.

So far, I seemed to be the only one to notice these small, telltale signs of a suffering which was getting worse and not better. Perhaps it was the mother in me, the mothering extending at times to this tall, serious girl whose own mother had proved herself worse than useless over the years. Annette Thomas had long ago taken herself off to Melbourne to live with her new partner, leaving her seventeen-year-old daughter who had just left school to fend for herself. Miranda had a brother, much older, married even then and living right up in Darwin. The father? A selfish, hedonistic womaniser who took off with his secretary, toured Europe on embezzled cash and eventually settled in Perth without ever being caught. Great family.

"Mum, you'll have to adopt Miranda now," Helen would joke.

The two girls had become friends in their first year at the Conservatorium, together with Gemma Smith and Jane Ellis. The "adoption" needed to be extremely subtle because Miranda had learnt very quickly to become self-sufficient and desperately needed to prove her independence. Uncomplaining, organised, hard-working and seemingly confident, she made a success of everything she did. It was left to me to spot the occasional glimpses of a fragility so successfully hidden from her own generation, but obvious to the watchful eyes of any discerning adult.

So many years later it is not my place now to sit in judgement upon Annette Thomas for a decision made for reasons she undoubtedly believed were valid at the time. Neither can I presume to understand the pressures that may have led her to this unfortunate choice. Yet even now, half a lifetime later, this strange woman continued to show scant interest in her lovely daughter, and even less in her adorable twin grandsons whom she hardly ever bothered with. Two or three phone calls a year fulfilled her maternal obligations. I found this situation utterly incomprehensible.

*

It was a week later, and the *Háry János Suite* scheduled again for rehearsal.

"Ten minute break," announced John Abbott, "and ten minutes only. We have a lot of work to get through tonight."

Grumbles all around, especially from the brass.

"We've played about two notes all night and now we're having a break. Why can't we just keep going and finish early?"

"Sorry, chaps. Strings need a breather. It's only a short interval tonight, as you heard. Anne, can you please make sure you ring the bell in ten minutes time?"

More grumbles, this time from the strings and winds who had been working their butts off for ninety minutes solid and thought they needed more than a lousy ten minutes to recover.

"Bugger him! Can't even get to the coffee in ten minutes," Miranda muttered irritably.

"Now, now, my dear, you mustn't fuss like that. It's really very naughty of you," a silky voice hissed in her ear. She swung round to see this squat little guy sidling up to her as close as he could manage without actually kicking her in the ankles.

"Oh hello, Frank," she replied wearily. "Just hope we actually get to the head of this damn queue before we all die of thirst."

"Actually, Miranda, I'm so glad I caught you just now. I've been wanting to have a word with you."

"Anything in particular?"

"Yes. Can you stay behind for a few minutes after we've finished tonight?"

"Well, I'm not sure, Frank. You see..."

The rest of her words were drowned in a sea of general chatter, then all too soon, the dreaded bell.

"Back to the salt mines," Abbott announced pleasantly.

The second half of the rehearsal began promptly. But all through it I puzzled over Sardor's strange request. I knew full well that it was none of my business but at the same time, I was feeling unusually protective of this lonely, sensitive girl, so badly and so recently hurt. What, if anything, was going on?

My ill-defined sense of unease returned with a sharpened intensity. And after a somewhat disturbed sleep, I decided the next morning that I must to do something about it. If I didn't, then who would?

Scene Three

Brisbane

The morning sun streamed across the balcony and through the multi-paned French doors of my upstairs music room. I love this bright, elegant room, my favourite place in the whole house. It was ten o'clock on a clear November day later in that same week and Miranda was due any minute now. The coffee was ready in the kitchen and freshly made scones sat cooling on their pretty enamel tray.

With a certain amount of guile I had rung Miranda to suggest going over our keyboard parts some time in order to compare notes and to see if the parts shared any themes in common. In actual fact, I had a pretty good idea that each keyboard part was completely independent, but thankfully Miranda fell for my ruse. I had also carefully chosen a day when I knew that Sarah would be out at her beloved bridge games. Now while Sarah is an utter darling, she simply cannot help wading into any delicate situation with great, clunking hob-nailed boots.

Miranda and I had our morning tea before working through each part for well over an hour, sitting together at my study table in the music room. Time then to test it on the two pianos. We found this exercise most enjoyable, giving us as it did, the chance to hear our parts with much greater clarity than could ever be possible when surrounded by the thick texture of the other instruments in a full rehearsal. At the end of it, Miranda stood up with a smile, stretched her long arms and yawned like a contented cat.

"Oh sorry! How rude of me!"

"Never mind. Sign of a good rehearsal. Nothing like a healthy yawn at the end of it to get some oxygen into the lungs again."

"Thanks. You know, I've really enjoyed this morning, Veronica."

"Me too. Time for another coffee?"

"Why not? The others are all at school and I'm not teaching until five this afternoon."

I settled back into my favourite chair. Time now to put my mind at rest, if possible.

"I see you have a not so secret admirer?" I smirked.

"Oh yeah? And who's the lucky guy?"

"It's none other than the glamorous European violinist. Frank someone or other."

"That creep? He had me bailed up for ten minutes the other night when I was itching to get home to bed."

"Yes, I overheard him chatting you up at the break. Was he trying to crack on to you, or something?"

"As if! No, what he apparently wants is not my body but my marvellous piano playing."

"Oh?"

"It seems that he's involved in some festival or other up the north coast. Wanted me to play the *Kreutzer* with him. In two weeks' time, would you believe?"

"The *Kreutzer*? He'd have to be off his head. No offence, Miranda, and I know you're a whiz-bang sight-reader. But even you couldn't learn the *Kreutzer* in a fortnight."

"Of course I couldn't. It's bloody ridiculous. You know, I read once that parts of it used to scare even the great accompanist Gerald Moore. Anyway, then when I knocked him back, he said, 'Well, what about the *Spring Sonata*?'"

"Good grief, that's almost as bad. I mean, it's a much less challenging work, but given that time frame, it's equally ridiculous."

"Trouble is, Veronica, he's done these sonatas on the violin about a hundred times each. And he's so arrogant and stupid that he thinks pianists can learn their thousands of notes in a tenth of the time it took him to learn his couple of hundred. It's so unfair."

"I know. Of course the really good string players all understand this, but you wouldn't believe the number of middling to good violinists who still think that all we have to do is to press buttons on a keyboard. Makes you sick... So the festival is off, for you at least?"

"No. I'm afraid I didn't get out of it that easily."

"Tell me the worst."

"It's really quite simple. In the end he settled for half a dozen violin 'lollies' that can be put together in a short time. Things like *Meditation*, some Fritz Kreisler pieces, some of the lighter Elgar violin works. You know, the sort of quite pretty stuff that always goes down well with a non-specialist audience. So in the end, I said 'Yes' mainly to get rid of him. Anyway it will do me good to get away for a weekend."

"Away? Where to?"

"Gympie. It's only overnight. The kids will be okay with their father."

We sat for a while in companionable silence. But I looked up a minute later, shocked to see her slumped in her armchair with a look of utter misery on her face.

"Okay, love. Let's have it."

"Sorry, it's nothing," she mumbled, looking away. "Just tired all of a sudden."

"Sure it's nothing, Miranda?"

Her lip trembled before the tears came, slowly at first, then filling big, brown eyes and splashing down hot, flushed cheeks. The words stuck in her throat.

"I just ... can't ... I can't..." Her thin body shook with sobs.

"Let it out now, love. Go on, have a good cry. Don't keep it all inside. It doesn't do you any good, you know."

I went over to her chair, holding her as I would have held my precious Helen when she was small and hurt. We stayed like that, comforter and comforted, for what seemed endless minutes. Gradually the tears subsided. Miranda gave herself a kind of mental shake, sat up and blew her nose.

"Oh, God. I don't know why I did that. I'm so sorry, Veronica."

"Darling, that was just what you needed. How long is it since you've had a really good cry?"

"I don't know," she sniffed. "I don't think I've ever cried just like that before."

She looked up, embarrassed. "You know, I can't give in to myself with the boys around. They're still too young to understand what's happened. They just sense that something is wrong because Mum and Dad don't seem to like each other much any more. And I will not collapse in front of HIM. Wouldn't give him the satisfaction."

I chose my next words with great care.

"Miranda, dear. Please tell me to mind my own business if you like, but do you think Michael regrets what he did?"

She thought for a minute. "Oh I suppose he does, in his own selfish way," she said disgustedly. "...I mean, yes, it's very inconvenient having your wife so mad at you all the time, isn't it? Yes, it's darned uncomfortable being kicked out into the study to sleep. And yes, it's embarrassing having people know you're like a randy teenager who can't keep his fly done up. But is he sorry? I really wouldn't know. Or care."

"Do you still love him?"

"Love him? Love that bastard? I hate his guts."

"Then that means you do love him, my dear."

Miranda looked up, incredulous.

"I admit it sounds stupid. But you see, hate is only the other side of love. The obverse of the selfsame coin."

I gave that a moment to sink in.

"Did you know what the opposite of love is? It's not hate. It's indifference."

Miranda sighed. "You know, he actually says he still loves me. Can you credit it?"

"Yes, I can. I can believe it. I know that Michael has been both stupid and unfaithful. What he did was inexcusable. But underneath it all, he's a good man. You can't believe this now. But please God, in time, you will."

"But I can't trust him, Veronica," her eyes filled with tears again, "I can't trust him any more. How can I ever be certain he won't do this to me again?"

"You can't, sweetie. You can't be certain of anything. I'm afraid that's just life. All we can ever do is to believe in those we love and hope that they live up to our trust the next time. What's the alternative?"

"I've sometimes thought of an alternative. But then I remember the boys. I couldn't do that to them, could I? Could I?"

ACT FOUR

Bribie and Brisbane

> "Full fathom five thy father lies
> Of his bones are coral made;
> Those are pearls that were his eyes;
> Nothing of him that doth fade
> But doth suffer a sea-change
> Into something rich and strange
> Sea-nymphs hourly ring his knell,
> Hark! Now I hear them – Ding dong bell."
> (*The Tempest,* Act One)

Scene One

Pumicestone Passage is a marine wonderland. Wide at its southern end as it merges with the choppy waters of Moreton Bay, it narrows sharply the further north you go until the island is a mere hundred yards from the mainland just opposite Caloundra. At low tide you could almost walk across on the sandbanks. Not surprisingly, the great explorer Matthew Flinders in 1799 mistook it for a river, believing that Bribie was a part of the mainland.

Exquisitely beautiful with the jagged peaks of the Glasshouse Mountains sometimes mirrored in the glassy waters at sunset, by day the turquoise sea laps the ragged shores of myriads of small, green islands – some named, like Parrot Island, Little Goat Island

and Thooloora Island – some thirty more, unnamed and uninhabited.

The passage teems with life. Dolphins, dugongs, migratory birds and seagulls all share their sacred territory with the boaties and fishermen who have come to relish this rare slice of heaven. Yet paradise comes with a price tag. Unwary voyagers who neglect to keep a sharp lookout for the constantly shifting sands can quickly find themselves firmly embedded for several hours until lifted off on the next high tide. Indeed, even a good "Brownie's" map and a vigilant attitude are not always proof against the whims of these capricious shallows, as I have learnt to my cost over many years of boating. Memories of straining to push a heavy aluminium hull through slimy, weed-encrusted sand and mud on hot summer days still make me wince.

These idle thoughts occupied me as I sat on the steps at White Patch enjoying my fish and chips. Today's visit to the island was a bonus in the middle of a busy working week. I had come up just for the day to do some much-needed gardening and tidying before the onslaught of the summer holidays. I decided to reward my efforts with lunch and a swim at my favourite part of the island.

The high tide lapped the lowest steps of the wooden staircase leading down to the narrow beach. I had just jumped in and swum out a few yards when I was startled by a dog barking from behind me. Turning round, I was surprised to see Seth and his canine friend sitting in their boat not twenty yards away, a slack line dangling in the water.

"Don't scare me fish," Seth growled companionably.

"Don't spoil my swim," I replied cheekily with a well-aimed splash towards the boat.

I turned over to float awhile. I never tire of this enchanted place. Towards the shoreline, thick clumps of Bribie pine trees paint their reflected colour on a smooth surface of clear, green water that is almost riverine. Once again, I am the child of an inland city, splashing in the shallows of the Bremer River, until I strike out to sea again towards the purple mountains on the distant mainland.

"Y'up for the holidays?"

"Afraid not. Just here for the day. Fish biting?"

"They were until you started makin' all that racket." Seth saw my stricken look.

"Only kiddin'. 'Ere. Look at this."

He held up a squirming bream in one hand while fending off the dog with the other.

"Not bad, eh? Got a whole bucketful. Keep me goin' for a week."

"What a life, Seth! I almost envy you."

"Ah well. Suits me. Couldn't stand going back, neither. Too many people. Hate crowds. Been on me own so long."

I tried to picture his eremitic lifestyle, seemingly idyllic, but exacting a price far beyond the reach of normal humanity. Constant loneliness, ever-present danger, endless solitude holed up on a tiny, mangrove-ridden speck in the middle of a vast seaway. How did this strange man survive all this?

"Yep, been 'ere a long time, but never get bored." Seth read my mind like an MRI. "So much to look at and all day to do it in ... 'ere, sit still, yer silly mutt, ya'll knock that bucket over. Take this and shut up." Buster, suitably chastened, subsided with a whimper before noisily attacking a large, meaty bone.

I swam a few lazy strokes around the boat. The water was like warm silk and I sank into its sensuous folds, enjoying a rare moment of mindless peace. But after a few minutes, a disturbing memory intruded this sacred space to jolt me back to reality.

"Seth," I said, swimming back to the boat, "I've just remembered something."

He looked up, surprised.

"A few weeks ago when I ran into you down here, you promised to tell me about some of the strange things you've seen over the years."

"I did, did I?"

"Yep."

"Gawd, I wouldn' know where to start. Reckon I could write a book..."

"Then just give me the first chapter. Please!"

"Okay. Need a fag first. Hold on."

Out came the ancient tin, tobacco papers, whole paraphernalia. Ceremony completed, Seth was ready to hold court. He settled back comfortably against the stern of the tinny, cigarette in one hand, fishing line still in the other.

"Yer know, I've seen some queer things in me time. Wrote some of 'em down over the years so I could remember 'em. But there's one thing I never had to write down. Stuck in me mind so fast I couldn't forget it if I tried."

"And why's that?"

"Listen and I'll tell yer... Okay. It were a long time ago. Dunno know just how long, but must have been close on forty year."

"You been here that long, Seth?"

"'Bout forty-five year, give or take ... anyway I don't remember the year exact, but I do know it was summer because it was stinkin' hot and I was out on the jetty with nothin' on but a pair of shorts and me old hat. I think I was fishin'. Anyway, that don't matter. I remember thinkin' that we might get a storm later on. Yer know that real close kind of day when yer feel yer can't hardly breathe? It was like that. So quiet yer could hear the fish plop jumpin' outta the water. No boats out, no nothin'. I know it was late mornin' because I remember thinkin' I should go in and get meself a feed. But just as I was thinkin' this, I heard ... Hey, mate, how well do yer know the Passage?"

"Pretty well, I'd say. Years ago, my husband and I had a small boat, and now my son-in-law has a tinny. I've explored it pretty well over the years."

"Righto. Well then, ye'll know that just before yer get to my place, the boat channel divides."

"Oh yes, I remember. The main channel is Gallagher gutter and it goes up past Gallagher Point on Bribie, but the other channel swings left past Little Goat Island and skims past Donnybrook on the mainland. Yes, I remember alright. James and I got stuck once on a sandbank in Dunlop's gutter just past Donnybrook. Took hours to get off. How could I ever forget?"

"Yer got the pitcher. Anyway, this day like I said, I was on the jetty when all of a sudden I 'ear this damn racket. Someone was cursin' and yellin' like yer wouldn't believe. I looked up and 'ere was this little wooden boat stuck like glue."

"But what's so unusual about that?"

"Stop interruptin', I'm goin' to tell yer ... I called out, 'Hold on and I'll give ya a shove'. But this weird character jus' shook his head. Wouldn't let me help, and him all alone with no other boats around neither. He waved me away and pushed the boat even harder, swearin' like a madman all the time. But then I seen a lady in the boat, too. So after a while he got her out and made her push with him. I called out again, 'That's no work for a lady,' but he just yelled at me to shut up and the two of 'em pushed and shoved like old Harry and managed to get it orf. That's the last I saw of 'em. For a while, anyway."

"What do you mean, 'for a while'?"

"Well, we DID get a storm, a real beauty. But it cleared pretty quick. Then late that afternoon, I was out in the boat fishin'. But this time I was on the other side of me island in that little gutter, Tony's gutter – yer know, the one that feeds into the main channel at Gallagher gutter."

I nodded.

"Ye're not goin' to believe this, but I seen the same boat headin' back towards the Bongaree end of Bribie."

"Seth, lots of people go up the passage one way and back down the other. What's so strange about that?"

"I'll tell yer what's strange, lady. That boat only had one person in it. Two went up, and one come back."

"Maybe the woman was lying down in the boat."

"Could be, but I don't think so. By then, the tide was in and there were no sandbanks between me and the other boat. I could see the bloke's face so clear – it was definitely the same person – and I could see some of the boat floor. I wouldn't swear to it, but if there was someone else in that boat, he must of shrunk her while he had lunch."

"Seth, just what are you saying?"

"Yer know what I'm sayin', only I won't never say it out loud. In case I'm wrong, see? That's why I never went to the police. Couldn't never be sure."

"You know what I think is really funny? Why was this chap so scared of you helping him? You know, when he was aground in the morning on the way up the passage."

"Yer got it, mate. He was terrified I'd come near him. Shit scared he was. And yer know somethin' else? I reckon he had it all planned out. Go up that inside passage where there aren't hardly any boats around, instead of goin' up the main passage which is much deeper. The main passage is much better boatin', especially when the tide's goin' out. Not that many sandbanks."

"But then, he hadn't planned on having you see him, had he? So he had to take the risk of going back on the main channel in case you noticed him again."

"Yair, that's right. And he didn't know I saw him again that time, neither. Smart arse probably thinks he got away with it."

I stood silently in the water for a minute, trying to take in this appalling tale.

"You know, Seth, there could be a perfectly innocent explanation."

"Like what?"

"Oh I don't know. Maybe the lady really was in the boat and you couldn't see her. Maybe she put to shore somewhere... No, that's silly. It's still uninhabited up there, isn't it? I mean, why would any man leave a woman alone in deserted places like Poverty Point, or even Mission Point which is accessible only by boat?"

"That's what I say, too. Especially then, when they didn't have no proper picnic places up there like there are now ... weird, I call it."

"Seth, I'll have to be getting back soon. I'm a bit cold now, anyway."

"Yair, I've had it for today, too. Got a good catch this mornin'. Need to get home and clean this lot before it goes orf... Funny old world, innit?"

"Funny isn't the word for it. Thanks for sharing this with me. Told anyone else?"

"Only one or two people, and they're kicked the bucket by now. Nobody wants to hear about somethin' that happened so long ago, I reckon."

"I guess that's right. 'Bye Seth. See you again."

'More things in Davy Jones' locker than you could poke a stick at.' I swam slowly up to the steps, dried myself off and drove back to the cottage, wondering just how well I'd sleep that night.

*

I slept very badly. Back home in Brisbane, two disparate themes kept circling in my head all night, round and round and round like some crazy rondo with Sections A and B but without a third tune to make Section C. Not surprisingly, theme A was my disturbing conversation with old Seth. That alone would have been enough to make me lose sleep.

But there was more. When I had gone back from White Patch to the cottage, I thought I'd just take another quick look at the old chest of drawers before heading home to beat the rush hour on the highway. And as I opened the second drawer to look for possible borers, I was surprised to see a newspaper cutting fall out and flutter down on to the bare boards of the back veranda. Of course, I remembered it now, but it was a couple of weeks since Andrew, Helen and I had first seen this ancient piece of reportage in *The Courier-Mail* and with so many more important things going on in our lives, I had naturally forgotten all about it. Now I looked more carefully ... "music student Heinrich Schwartzkopf whose body was retrieved from the Salzach River, Salzburg in the early hours of ..."

So here it comes, theme B of my nocturnal rondo – an unwelcome guest stubbornly insinuating itself into my half-conscious mind and refusing to budge as it writhed and twisted its loathsome message around theme A to create a crazy rhythm which could have no possible meaning.

"Two went up and one come back ... two went up and one come back... Body retrieved from the Salzach River... Body retrieved from the Salzach River. Full fathom five thy father lies. Full fathom... Oh shut up, for heaven's sake! ... JUST SHUT UP! I need my sleep."

Scene Two

Brisbane

I stumbled out into the kitchen the next morning at the unheard of hour of eight o'clock to find Sarah already halfway through *The Courier-Mail* crossword, an empty coffee cup at her elbow.

"Well, you're alive at last! I was just about to ring for an ambulance."

"Had a restless night," I yawned.

"Bad dreams?"

"You might call it that. Just say I had something on my mind."

"What?"

"I'm worried about Miranda," I replied, deciding to tell the truth but not the whole truth.

Well, I was worried about her, but just not last night. However, I wasn't about to unleash any wild nocturnal fantasies upon my pessimistic sister. Sarah's dark Celtic imagination always works overtime, and I didn't need her superstition to add to my growing sense of unease about something I couldn't yet even begin to understand.

My sister got up and refilled her cup.

"Anything we can do to help?" she asked, steady blue eyes full of concern.

I patted her on the shoulder as I went over to the pantry to get my breakfast muësli.

"Yes, I think there is, dear heart. I'm going to find out all I can about this creep that's been pestering her."

"You mean that odd violinist you mentioned?"

"Yes, him."

"But why him, Veronica? He's probably just a bit eccentric. Like most musicians I know."

She ducked just in time to avoid the playful swipe I aimed at her left ear.

"I'll ignore that crack. No, seriously, I just feel that he's something a bit more than merely eccentric. He's ... I don't know. Somehow unwholesome."

"And you think he's some kind of threat to that poor girl?"

"I certainly hope not. But that's what I intend to find out. Did you know he's going to Gympie next weekend with Miranda? They're performing at some local festival."

"Well, in that case, I suppose you can't be too careful, then. And exactly what plans do you have in mind, Sherlock Holmes?"

"I'm going to ring Andrew. He worked with Sardor in the State Orchestra before he retired from full-time playing. He might know something."

*

I was sitting in a very popular café near the roundabout at West End three days later. Andrew had arranged to meet me there during his rehearsal break. With his usual sharp sensitivity, he had sensed my concern during our phone conversation.

"Sorry to drag you away when your break time is so precious, but I didn't want Helen to know. At least not at this early stage," I apologised.

"Fair enough, Veronica. You know, she still has the occasional flashback, but only when something like this crops up to remind her."

I nodded. Andrew is a wonderful young man, impossible to dislike in any case. But between this mother-in-law and son-in-law there exists a bond that goes far beyond the usual ties of acquired kinship. Instead, we enjoy a unique friendship, a mutually deep affection born in shared anxiety and forged like steel in the crucible of a hideous flight to London as we sat together through an endless night, not knowing if the girl we both loved so much would even be alive to greet us."

"Helen's fine now, thank God. After all these years."

"Sixteen years." I wrenched my mind back to the present. "I wish I could say the same about Miranda."

"Me too. Anyway, you asked me for a low-down on Frank."

"The low-down on the lowlife."

Andrew grinned.

"You'll have to go to Confession now, dear Ma-in-law. Anyway, I did a bit of snooping about my esteemed ex-colleague. Of course he played with us for years, but you don't always get to know people in the other sections that much unless you happen to mix with them socially."

"Anything you've got will be a help."

"Well, I do know this much. He's Hungarian. Not sure just what his musical background is except that he's quite a competent orchestral player without being anything out of the ordinary."

"Helen seems to think he's very ambitious. Apparently he's started throwing his weight around a bit now that he's playing in a community orchestra. Seems to think he's God's gift to the Morelands Symphony. He even tries to embarrass the conductor at rehearsals. You know, calling out all the time and making a complete fool of himself."

"That'd be right. Always was a bit of an upstart. You know the type. Name-dropping, constantly trying to make out he's better than he actually is. Of course this didn't affect me at all, not having to put up with his antics in the same section. But Mark – Mark Simpson, Gemma's husband in the violas, used to end up sitting near the seconds sometimes and found him a complete arsehole."

"So he usually played second violin?"

"Mostly. That's why his posturing and his rubbish were so pathetic. He thought he was Zuckerman. But wait, there's more."

"Oh?"

"Well, as you know, lots of people have enlarged egos, which is very annoying, but probably harmless enough. However, this dude happens to be carrying around quite a bit of excess baggage and some of it isn't so nice."

"Don't keep me in suspense, Andrew. I'm really worried about Miranda."

"I know you are. We all are. Anyhow, it seems that our dear little friend was up on an assault charge years ago."

"What?"

"Yep! He's been married twice. No info about wife number one, but apparently he used to get stuck into wife number two. Did it once too often. She upped and left, but not without first going to the police and getting a restraining order against him."

"Was he convicted?"

"Unfortunately no. You know just how hard it is sometimes to get conclusive evidence. Anyway, he's been single ever since. Which probably explains the next thing."

"There's more?"

"Afraid so. It would appear – and my sources are pretty reliable – that our darling Franky likes the Internet. He likes it a lot. Particularly some of the nastier porn sites."

"You mean the ones that are really perverted? Even violent?"

"Looks like it."

I sat there trying to digest this latest piece of loathsome information. No wonder I had felt such revulsion the first time I had laid eyes on him when he was ogling Miranda. Nasty little baggage.

"You know Miranda's doing a gig with him next weekend, don't you? That's why I'm so worried."

"No, I didn't, Veronica. Helen and I are both so busy that sometimes we just bump into each other in doorways and it's days before we exchange any news more significant than 'Could you put petrol in the car tomorrow, love?' or 'Who's taking Clare to netball on Saturday?'"

I smiled. Truly, the young parents of today have it hard.

"Well at least we are forewarned. And I don't suppose Miranda can come to any harm. I mean, he's not exactly going to bash her up on stage, is he?"

Andrew looked thoughtful for a minute.

"No, I guess you're right, Veronica. But just the same, it wouldn't hurt to put her on her guard. If you can do it somehow without scaring her to death."

"I'll certainly try."

"If anyone can do it, my dear extra mother, it will be you. Meanwhile I'll keep digging."

Well, I did try to warn her a few days later. Without much luck.

"I'll be okay, Veronica," she shrugged, the dull expression in her eyes and the dejected posture telling another story.

Miranda couldn't care less. Quite simply, she had given up.

London – 1958

He really did feel he had a reason to kill Abbott now. To be sure, the rough ride that had lasted nearly a year had so accustomed him to the daily irritation of this burr in the saddle that he almost enjoyed the sensation. In some perverse way, it had felt so good to hate. But this was different. A particular event in the last week of term had begun to fan the embers of this smouldering resentment into a red hot flame of anger, an anger he hadn't felt so acutely since being forced to leave Austria.

It was graduation week, the final students' concert of the academic year. Sardor's results in this first year of study had been good – indeed, they were especially praiseworthy in view of the immense cultural and language difficulties he had had to overcome in such a short time. He had every reason to be proud of his efforts. But he wasn't proud of them at all. Instead, he fumed at the huge injustice of it, for no matter how hard he tried, there was always someone better than him. Such humiliation was insupportable.

The graduation concert was in full swing and was now into its second half. John Abbott strode across the stage, bowed gracefully to the audience, sat down at the piano and adjusted the stool. The student orchestra struck up the first exquisite bars of Mozart's "Coronation Concerto". Abbott was completely relaxed during the long orchestral introductory tutti, even smiling to himself a little as he hummed some of the themes under his breath and blissfully oblivious of Sardor glowering at him from his desk in the second violins. How unjust it all was. Here was this pampered milksop reared in the lap of luxury, now unashamedly wallowing as a soloist in the admiration of a rapt audience while he, Frank Sardor, was mere orchestral fodder. What did Abbott know of hardship, of fear, of mind-numbing exhaustion? Had he ever been so hungry that he'd eat even the rancid, day-old scraps spilling out of the skip in the laneway behind the restaurant kitchen? Had he ever seen his favourite cousin bundled into a van at midnight and taken away? Had he ever been so petrified that the top half of his body was frozen into immobility while his bladder relaxed and emptied its contents all over the road? The hell he had!

The first movement of the concerto had finished now. The applause was thunderous. The orchestra was dispersing to make way for the dignitaries processing up to their chairs on the platform for the prize giving. Sardor looked up from his seat in the audience just in time to see John Abbott swaggering across the stage ready to receive the prize for the most outstanding student of his year. It was not to be borne.

*

But much worse was to follow. Just a few months before Christmas, to his delighted surprise, Sardor had actually managed to acquire a girlfriend. She was a fellow Hungarian equally lonely in a new country, equally ill at ease with the unfamiliarity of so many customs that seemed strange and uncongenial. At first the relationship was just an acquaintanceship, a mutual sharing of ideas and experiences made all the more enjoyable for being expressed in their own language. Soon the friendship had turned to something much deeper. If not a passionate love, then at least it was a strong mutual affection.

They were married on Christmas Eve, the thick, white flakes of snow falling with a gentle softness on Maria's dark hair as they walked laughing, hand in hand out the Registry Office door and into the maelstrom of Marylebone Road. At last, he was happy.

*

But his happiness didn't last. Something happened soon afterwards to ruin everything. The event in itself was quite trivial; the innocent perpetrator apologised and said that he had meant no harm. Sardor refused to believe him. It felt better that way.

It was like this. New Year, the most dismal of all seasons in these damp, bleak islands. Staff and students at the Royal College of Music were indulging in the national pastime of complaining about the rotten weather, the end of the short Christmas holidays and anything else they could find to bitch about to liven the midwinter gloom. Sardor had just come out of the studio from his first violin lesson after the holidays and was walking down the passageway when he saw them. Maria, sitting in the common area reading quietly and someone he didn't want to see coming towards her from the opposite direction. Instinctively, he shrank back out of sight behind a post, the old furtive habit of years returning in a flash.

"Cold enough for you, is it sweetheart?" Abbott asked cheerily, sitting down beside Maria, a shade too close.

She smiled non-committally.

"Here. We can't have that, you know." He reached out and held her hand. "Your tiny hand is frozen, let me warm it into life," he sang in a passable rendition of the famous tenor aria from La Bohème.

Maria laughed as she pulled her hand away. "John, you can't do that now. Look at my other hand."

"Hell! You're MARRIED? When?"

"Just before the holidays. It was Christmas Eve. I don't suppose many people here would know about it yet."

"Well, I'm blowed. Anyway, congratulations, gorgeous. And who's the lucky man?"

"Frank Sardor."

"Oh ... that's a bit of a surprise. Well, all the very best. I suppose I'll have to find someone else to flirt with now, won't I?" He laughed good-naturedly as he stood up and resumed his promenading along the corridor. Unable to continue skulking behind the pillar any longer, Sardor stepped out from his hiding place scowling like a spoilt teenager.

"I say old chap, you've been and gone and done it now. Congrats and all that." Abbott gave him a friendly slap on the shoulder.

"Thank you," Sardor replied stiffly.

"Sorry I flirted with your wife. Didn't know she'd tied the knot." He walked off jauntily, whistling the rest of the Bohème aria under his breath.

A huge black hole was opening up under Sardor's feet. It was obvious that he couldn't trust anybody now. That detestable lecher who had probably already bedded half the female student population was starting on his wife. And if it came to that, could Maria herself even be trusted? The way she had simpered and giggled at Abbott when he was singing that ridiculous song made her look as if she was actually enjoying it. Little bitch. She would need a good talking to. Immediately.

Meanwhile, he had Abbott to deal with. One way or another, he was going to pay. Even if it took a lifetime.

*

Scene Three

Brisbane

A hot, sticky night at the end of November, with the threat of a late storm. I was just getting ready for the second last rehearsal of the Morelands Symphony when the phone rang.

"Oh hello, Mum. Sorry to be ringing so late but change of plan." Helen sounded rushed and out of breath.

"Slow down, little one. What's up?"

"Well, you couldn't have known it, but Andrew has to work tonight. It's a royal pain in the butt. Someone's sick, which means that at the last minute he has to fill in and do the ballet tonight as well as tomorrow."

"Right. So now you have baby-sitting problems? Do you want Sarah to mind them?"

"We thought of that, but Gemma offered to have the kids over at her place. You know how she loves our three."

"That's nice of her."

Gemma Smith was a violinist and one of Helen's best friends at the Con. She did so well at her studies that she had got a job straight after graduation playing in the State Orchestra. Though she had always longed for a husband and family, she remained single for many years, seemingly unable to find "the right man" until years later when a colleague was tragically widowed. Left alone to bring up his two little girls, violist Mark Simpson struggled with work and home as only a single parent can. Nobody was surprised when Gemma, with her typical kindness and concern, stepped in to help with Brighid and Caitlin. The resulting scenario surprised her friends even less. Now happily married for two years, Gemma revelled in her instant family which had recently grown with the addition of baby Jack.

"Anyway, Mum," Helen continued, "I'm sorry, but this means that we won't have time to take the kids over to Bardon and then drive back to pick you up. I really hate to put you out but it's so much easier for us to take our three over to the Simpsons' on our way than to ask poor old Gemma to uproot the baby at night and bring him over here. Plus our three can do their homework there."

"You don't have to apologise, love. I'm quite capable of driving to rehearsal on my own. So I guess Andrew will pick you up after our rehearsal on his way home from the ballet?"

"Got it in one, Mother dear... Oh God, look at the time. And I haven't even packed my cello yet."

"No, and I'm not dressed either. See you there, sweetie."

*

There was something very peculiar about Miranda that night. Sadly, we had all become accustomed over the last month to seeing her depressed, moody, withdrawn even. But this was different again. Instead of the lethargy which she habitually wore now like a moth-eaten old cloak, tonight she was noticeably jumpy, hyperactive, twitchy. Occasionally she would look anxiously over her shoulder like the poor Ancient Mariner, as if she were seeing some invisible spook. What on earth was going on?

I managed to corner Helen at the break, dragging her over to a quiet spot in the hall away from the crowd.

"Have you been watching Miranda tonight?"

"Not really. I'm on the other end of the stage from the piano, remember. Why?"

"She's been like a cat on hot bricks the whole time. She's even missed a couple of important entries. And what's more... Good Lord! There's Michael."

"Where?"

"Don't turn round now, but when you can, sneak a look over there... He's just walked in and he's standing with his arm around her."

"Hell!"

"I can't believe my eyes."

"Me neither... But you know, Mum, just as we were coming in tonight she bumped into me in the passageway. Said that something dreadful had happened over the weekend but that it was probably an ill wind because it had brought Michael back to her."

"What sort of an ill wind?"

"Don't know. She couldn't say any more because there was a whole pile of violins walking right behind us... Oh bugger! There's the bell already."

"OK. Catch you before we go home."

*

But we didn't meet up after all. Because our concert was only two weeks away, at this rehearsal John was unusually meticulous, going over and over things, trying to get everything just right before the big day. To our collective disgust, we were still there well after our usual ten o'clock finishing time. "Anyone who really needs to go, please go quietly." So it was that Helen looked up in mid phrase to see Andrew standing patiently at the back of the hall. With a whispered apology to her desk partner, she gathered cello, bow and music folder and hurried off to pack up. No such luck for me. We were still doing *Háry János* in which both Miranda's part and mine were important. Finally at twenty past ten, Abbott called it a night, apologising for the late finish.

I had to get off that stage fast. How else could I avoid Miranda? I had no wish to intrude into a sensitive situation. I managed to achieve a quick vanishing act out to the car park, ready for a speedy get away. Miranda and her problems would doubtless catch up with me soon enough.

Damn! Someone had parked me in. It had to be an orchestra member. All the other groups that use the Old Museum building had long since departed. Well anyway, I wouldn't have long to wait unless the owner of HUN 56 happened to get held up putting away music stands, in which case I would be stuck there for another quarter of an hour. My night time cocoa ritual with Sarah would just have to wait.

I had barely got into my car when I saw them come out. Frank Sardor trying to melt into the brickwork. Following close on his heels, Michael, holding Miranda's hand.

"Over here, Sardor," Michael's voice, low, but quite audible through my car window.

"I SAID, over here." Reluctantly, Sardor swung around.

"I want to talk to you."

I shrank down quickly behind my dashboard just as they all walked past to the other side of the garden bed. I had no choice but to eavesdrop, trapped as I was behind that blasted Corolla.

"Yess," hissed Sardor, "and what is it you want? My time is preciouss."

"So's my wife."

"Michael."

"No, love. Let me sort this out. The bastard's not getting away with it."

"You insult me like this and I'll..."

"You'll do nothing, you disgusting piece of vermin. I'd like to knock you and your stupid glasses right back to Budapest, except that I wouldn't dirty my hands on garbage like you."

"How dare you! A musician of my standing with..."

"What standing? You're just a second-rate, jumped-up, arrogant has-been. I've heard all about you and the rubbish you carry on with. Anyway I don't care who the hell you think you are, just leave my wife alone or you'll curse the day you were ever born...

And now get out of my sight before I really lose my temper and kick you arse over tit into those rose bushes."

Shivers! This was a Michael I had never encountered before. How on earth was I going to escape unnoticed now?

A crunch of feet on the gravel heralded a furious Sardor marching, unseeing, past my car, barging into the Corolla and slamming the door. So that's the selfish cow who had parked me in. I was hastily starting my own car when a soft knock on the window made me look up.

"Sorry about this, Veronica."

"Michael." I recovered my wits quickly. "Whatever it is, it's none of my business."

"Yes it is, Veronica." Miranda interposed. "You've been so kind and so concerned for me in all of this, you deserve an explanation. "

"Well, only when you're ready, dear. Anyway, seeing you both back together again makes it all worthwhile, doesn't it?"

Miranda gave a rueful laugh.

"I suppose you might say that." She looked affectionately at Michael. "It's very late now. I'll give you a ring soon, Veronica. Promise."

Scene Four

Brisbane

The next few days passed in a flurry of teaching, giving extra lessons to my piano exam candidates, and practising for not only the *Háry János* but for three of Helen's cello students who had their string exams coming up soon.

"I know this seems mad, Mum," Helen had apologised a few weeks beforehand, "I mean, I always do these kids' accompaniments myself, as you know, but I'm absolutely flat strapped at the moment. Gemma and I are playing at a fund-raising soirée at her place next month and I'm trying to learn the piano part of the *Spring Sonata* to play with her. Only the first movement, but it's still a fair bit of work. Plus all this cello stuff for our Morelands concert. It's too much. Would you be an angel and accompany my three babies, just this once? You'd save my life if you could."

Of course I could. I adore accompanying and jump at every chance I get. So it was that I was right in the middle of wrestling with *Kol Nidrei* when the ringing of the phone pulled me up short. Miranda, calling as promised.

*

"Are you sure you want to talk about all this, dear?"

Miranda nodded. "I really don't know quite where to start." Her hands were shaking as she put down her coffee cup.

I patted her on the shoulder. "Then let me help you a little... Something happened in Gympie? With that creep you did the concert with?"

"Yes. Oh Veronica, it was awful. It was..."

"Take your time, love. I have all afternoon. I've only got one student and she's not coming until six o'clock." I tried not to think of the two hours I had put aside for practice today. I'd make it up somehow.

"Well, it was like this. We did the concert and it all went pretty well. The audience liked it anyhow. But then when we went back to the motel, he insisted on walking me right to my door. So far so good. But then..."

"Then he asked you if you'd like to come to his room for a drink."

"Veronica, you're psychic."

"No dear. Only old and jaded and worldly wise."

She smiled. "I didn't want to be rude, but I must have been an idiot not to see what he was up to. I guess I'm really not used to this sort of thing. Not any more. I mean, you know how it is. You've been married for X number of years, it's centuries since any man other than your husband has ever made a real pass at you and I suppose it just sort of ... takes you by surprise. Well, anyhow, it did with me."

"What happened next?"

"He went over to the bar fridge. *Oh dear! I don't seem to have anything left. I must have drunk the last beer just before the concert.* He turned around from the fridge and he had this lecherous smirk all over his face. More like a leer. It was the most disgusting thing I've ever seen in my life."

"Well, he's not exactly Mr Universe to start with is he?"

Miranda managed a grin. "He's REVOLTING, Veronica. As you know. Anyhow, I started to back off but he followed me. I ended up in a corner of the room squashed up against his horrible beer belly. I couldn't breathe. Then..."

"Take your time, dear."

"Then he began reaching for my boobs. Had his pudgy little hands all over me. I asked him to stop, but he just kept going. *I've wanted to do this ever since I first saw you,* he breathed. He stank of garlic and old cabbage. I started to get really scared then. I know you had tried to warn me, but at the time I simply couldn't take it in. I suppose I was too sunk in my own misery and self pity to take anything in at all."

"I did tell you that years ago he was apprehended for violence against his wife, didn't I?"

"Yes, you did. And when I remembered it, I was absolutely terrified. Thought he was going to rape me. Or worse."

"He probably was."

"Well, I decided that if so, this was the last thing he'd ever do. After what I'd been through all those weeks with Michael, I wasn't going to let yet another man treat me like dirt."

"Michael isn't a rapist," I murmured.

"I know that," Miranda snapped, "but you know what I mean, Veronica. Oh I'm sorry. I'm explaining myself very badly. What I'm trying to say is that I felt I'd had men up to here and this one wasn't going make me suffer any more."

"So what did you do?"

"I kneed him in the groin. Nice and hard."

"Good heavens!"

"I never thought I could do something like that."

"I can't imagine it, either. What next?"

"Well, of course he just collapsed with the pain. I must have had a good aim, mustn't I? Anyway when he was all doubled over, I made extra sure of things by giving him a smack across the jaw that he wouldn't forget in a hurry. He fell backwards on to the bed. I knew this was my only chance so I raced out the door, back to my own room and locked myself in."

"You must have been terrified."

"You bet I was. My heart was going like a hammer, I was gasping for breath and shaking like you wouldn't believe."

"Did you call the police? Or the motel management?"

"No I didn't. Funny, isn't it? My one thought was, *I've got to get out of here. I've got to get away from him. I've got to get home. NOW.* So I packed up like a lunatic, terrified the whole time that I'd hear him banging on the door. In ten minutes I was in the car. I drove like a maniac for that first half hour."

I must have looked rather disapproving.

"I know, Veronica. I know what you must be thinking. And I agree. I probably shouldn't have been even on the road in that condition. But I wasn't thinking clearly. It was like some animal instinct was taking over. I felt I was fleeing for my life."

"What time would all this have been?"

"Must have been about midnight by then. Luckily there was hardly any traffic on the road. Or else angels were looking after me. I don't know. Most of that journey remains a blur in my mind, even now. What I do remember is getting home at about two in the morning and banging on the door in a frenzy because I couldn't find my key and I had this crazy feeling that he was still out there after me. Of course Michael nearly collapsed with fright when he saw me appearing on the doorstep looking like a ghost. Thought I'd had a bad accident or was very sick."

"Gosh! How awful! No wonder you wanted to avoid the creature at the last rehearsal."

Miranda was quiet for a moment.

"You know, Veronica. The thing that makes it all so weird is that Michael had made me do a self defence course only last year. I hadn't wanted to, but he made me do it. If he hadn't…"

"If he hadn't, you mightn't have been sitting safely in this room right now telling me all about it."

"I know. And I feel I really owe my life to Michael. Or at the very least, I owe him my escape from an almost certain rape and beating up. That's why…"

"That's why you finally found yourself able to forgive him? After what he had done to you?"

Miranda sighed.

"Something like that. But not just that. It was also … it was also the feeling that what he had done, bad and all as it was, just paled into insignificance beside what Sardor had tried to do. It's hard to explain, but ... it was like a kind of revelation that life is too short to keep on hating a person forever. And somehow, I believed for the first time ever, that Michael was genuinely sorry; that he had been remorseful since the very moment it had happened. I felt that he – both of us – deserved another chance. Do you think I'm a fool for doing this, Veronica?"

"What I think is that this is perhaps the wisest thing you've ever done in your life so far."

I got up and stretched my cramped limbs. "I don't know about you, my dear girl, but after hearing all that, I need another coffee."

Miranda sat staring moodily into the dregs of her third cup of coffee.

"What else is it, sweetie?"

"Oh, it's probably nothing."

"It's never just nothing. Tell me."

"Well, it's just that I have to go back to Gympie again."

I looked up quickly.

"No, Veronica, it's not some unhealthy wish to revisit the scene of the crime, or anything morbid like that. I'm not that bad yet. Actually I think I'm holding together pretty well. What's happening is that I've got some examining to do up there in a couple of weeks. Just the very next day after the Morelands concert, as a matter of fact. Not good timing, is it, but you know what our job is like. Either a feast or a famine. Anyway I was scheduled for this Wide Bay session before I even knew about the festival gig in Gympie. Besides, it's only for two days and there are some Diploma exams thrown in."

"That's always a bit of a drawcard."

"I know it is. And I'm quite looking forward to it. It's just that…"

"That it's Gympie. I understand."

Miranda shuddered. "Oh, I know this is silly, but when I even begin to think about staying by myself in a motel, it brings it all back. I really feel I can't face it. I don't know what to do."

I thought for a minute. "Couldn't Michael go with you? Helen and Andrew would look after the boys for two days and surely Michael could ask for the Monday off, as special leave?"

"I know, we did think of all that. But Michael can't possibly get away just then. He has a choral festival all that Sunday. Four of his school choirs are competing. He hasn't a hope of getting out of it."

"Oh dear!"

For once, I felt I was stumped. Damnation! There had to be a way out.

"Got it!" I exclaimed a minute later.

Miranda sat up and laughed in spite of herself. "There's just no stopping you Veronica, is there? What's your bright idea, then?"

"Well, you probably don't know this, but many years ago before I was married, I used to teach in Gympie."

"I didn't know that. I mean, I knew you'd taught in quite a few places, but I hadn't heard of you teaching there. So how does this help me?"

"It was a long time ago now, but for four years I boarded with my uncle who owned a furniture and hardware shop right in the middle of town. The shop was up at the top end of Mary Street just before it intersects with Channon Street. The business was housed in an old building dating from Victorian times, possibly built just after the gold rush. I don't know for sure. Anyway, it's an interesting place. Walls about a foot thick and as solid as a rock. The shop itself occupies the ground floor. Upstairs there is a very comfortable flat, actually more like a house in size. Quite spacious with three bedrooms and a lovely old wrought-iron veranda looking out over the street. I used to love being out there during storms, watching the rain pouring down the bitumen and splashing in the gutters. I still remember the distinctive sound of the rain drumming on the iron roof... Anyway, that's all ancient history."

"Gosh, Veronica. You've got me fascinated."

"Well of course my uncle is long since gone to his eternal reward but the building is still in the family although the shop is now some sort of a garden supply business. My cousin Alan is the landlord. The flat is usually permanently let, but I know it's between tenants at the moment. The next lot aren't due in for another month. Alan likes to give the place a thorough going over between tenants and he had a bit of maintenance work to do this time after the last lot left it in quite a mess."

"What are you suggesting, Veronica?"

"I was wondering if you'd like to stay there for the two days. I know Alan would be delighted to put you up. He and his wife, Jane, would make sure the place was comfortable for you. A bed made up, basic items in the fridge, that sort of thing. You'd be right in the centre of town, close to everything and you'd have the place all to yourself after shop hours. No drunk footballers tramping past your door late at night, as so often happens in country motels. There's an on-site caretaker in the office building next door, so you couldn't be safer. And Alan is just a phone call away. What do you think, Miranda?"

"I think you're a bloody genius, Veronica. But then we all know that, don't we?"

"Stop, stop. It'll go to my head. Anyway, if you're agreeable, I'll ring Alan tonight and arrange it all. I really think you'd be much happier there than in a motel, especially after your horrible night there last week."

A visibly relieved Miranda was just getting up to go when I was assailed by a totally unconnected thought. Something that for days had been lodging as an unwelcome guest in the back of my mind suddenly swaggered forwards into consciousness.

"Oh Miranda, just before you leave, answer me this. The other night in the car park I noticed the number plate on Sardor's Corolla. It struck me because it was so distinctive."

Miranda chuckled. "You're referring to HUN56 I presume? Yes, it's distinctive all right. Rather hits you in the eye, doesn't it?"

"Sure does, but do you know why? Did you ever happen to ask him?"

"Ask him? You don't ask Sardor things like that, he just tells you in the first five seconds in case you've happened not to notice his stunning cleverness."

"So?"

"Well, the HUN is obvious because he really is Hungarian. 1956 is the year of the Hungarian revolution, as you know. He managed to escape to Austria and I think he spent a few years in England before he got the job here in the State Orchestra. Anyway, he said he chose 1956 as a tribute to so many he knew who had died in the revolution. "

"Sounds quite touching. But can you believe him?"

"As a matter of fact, Veronica, I do. We know he's a disgusting, arrogant sleaze. But I really don't think he's a liar. At least, I don't think he's lying in this case. Why are you so interested?"

"Oh … just wondering," I replied casually.

Brisbane- November 2004

He would have to skip the next rehearsal, even though it was the last one before the concert. That Neanderthal thug, Michael Healy, was far too dangerous. For a start, he was about twice Sardor's size and half his age. If they ever met again, Healy would be certain to get quite nasty and apart from the unthinkable humiliation of having to face his victor once again, the older man had no doubt about just who would come off second best if push came to shove. Like all bullies, Sardor was basically a coward.

Miranda, however, was a different kettle of fish. He wasn't remotely scared of her. The tough, little bitch had taken him completely by surprise that embarrassing night in Gympie. She had got the better of him, and nobody did this and got away with it. The next time, he would be ready for her, now that he knew all her little tricks. He would arrange it carefully so that there would be no witnesses. It would only be her word against his – and who would believe the word of an unstable woman suffering from depression? He just had to make sure he got her entirely on her own – sooner or later, it didn't matter when. All he had to do was wait.

But then there was Abbott. He had been free of this nemesis for the past forty years, only to have the detestable creature follow him halfway around the world and end up in not only the same city but in the same bloody orchestra. He just couldn't win.
"It isn't! No, it can't be! Not Frank Sardor?"
The Hungarian swung round, unable at first to place the voice.
"Yess, I am Frank Sardor."
"Well, well, what a small world! It's so good to see you after all these years. Sorry to have to rush, but I'm running a bit late.

Rehearsal starts in five minutes and I'm not ready yet. We'll catch up soon.''

Catching up was the last thing Sardor had wanted. He still loathed the man. The old, bitter memories came flooding back at that very first rehearsal like a tide of dirty water. Yet as it happened, he was the one to arrange a meeting, out of sheer necessity, nothing more. He had to see Abbott, and soon.

The reason for this was urgent. Weeks ago, Sardor had put his name forward to perform the Bartók Violin Concerto No. 2 with the orchestra. After all, it was an all Hungarian program, and who better than himself as a Hungarian national to be soloist? He knew he could play the piece, he had done it before. It was a sure thing. But to his disgusted amazement, the committee had knocked him back. He couldn't believe it. Unfortunately, his application had been presented far too late. The advertising had already gone out and the program couldn't be changed at this stage.

He seethed for days afterwards. How monstrously unfair, how like his usual rotten luck. It was nothing but stupid, small-minded protocol, so typical of these tin-pot community groups. But hold on! Maybe there was still a chance after all. This was not a professional body like the State Orchestra with its schedules arranged as far back as the previous year. The Morelands Symphony was a much smaller affair, and bound to be more flexible. He would swallow his resentment and approach John Abbott. As conductor he'd undoubtedly have the final say.

How wrong he was.

"Sorry old chap," Abbott had replied pleasantly, "I'd like to help, if only for old times' sake, and I'm quite sure you're up to the mark. But as guest conductor I'm afraid I have absolutely no say at all in choosing program items. I just come along and help perform what's been already planned. Why not apply again for next year?"

Why not? Because this concert is the one with the special Hungarian program, you useless, puffed up twit. Next year *wouldn't be the same at all. If you really wanted to, you could at least include one movement of the concerto. And anyway, I refuse to grovel – to you, to the committee or to anyone else. I've been rejected once. I'm not going to embarrass myself again.*

And so the dreary weeks ground on and on. To add to his bitter disappointment, Sardor was becoming increasingly irritated at Abbott's conducting. Like some orchestral players of the old school, he was convinced he could do a much better job than the marionette out front jerking the strings. Besides, it was obvious that this particular puppet master had very little feeling for Hungarian music. It was up to him, Frank Sardor, to correct him. To put him on the right path. To show him how it should be done. But again, he drew a blank.

"I know that players often have their own ideas, Frank, and I understand that you have a good feel for the music of your own countrymen," Abbott explained, this time with a touch of impatience, "but I'm afraid that on this ship, I am captain for the voyage. Like it or not, you're all stuck with my interpretation. Now I really must grab a coffee before the end of the break. Sorry to be a bit dismissive."

*

So nothing had changed. It was almost half a century later and yet he, Frank Sardor, was still on the receiving end of Abbott's unbearable superiority, his self-satisfied demeanour, his insufferable condescension. And despite Sardor's success in holding down an honourable position in a fine professional orchestra for so many years, he was still only a rank and file player, although a good one. He was not a star. He would never be a star. Not even a small star like John Abbott.

And then he remembered that matter of Maria. It was all so long ago, but nevertheless the humiliating event which had been securely buried together with a myriad of other painful memories was rising now to the surface of his consciousness like scum on a stagnant pond. Abbott was fully accountable. It was his selfish, shameless flirtation so soon after the marriage that had planted the fertile seed of his wife's disillusionment with her new husband. Things had soured from that day forwards.

Of course it was all Abbott's fault. So he would have to get even; he would have to redress the balance. But how? It could be nothing remotely obvious. No violence this time. He had learnt his lesson the hard way. This time, the revenge had to be subtle, effective and completely untraceable.

Finally he had it. The car. Some time after the concert, he would tamper with Abbott's car. He was a skilled amateur mechanic and he knew he could do it all in such a way that his victim would be at the very least, severely inconvenienced, perhaps even injured. Injured, not killed. Death was not on his agenda. Yet if the worst did actually happen and Abbott were to die as a result, then what would that be but mere collateral damage? It would be no more than the skunk deserved.

He smiled to himself as he began planning.

*

Scene Five

Brisbane

The final rehearsal of the Morelands Symphony. Thank God. Much as I love playing, it was all getting a bit much. Musicians usually feel utterly flattened by November, and the hot weather doesn't help, either. Still, we had the concert next week to look forward to and doubtless that would shake us from our end of year lethargy.

Miranda and I happened to get to the hall a little ahead of everyone else.

"Well, the flat's all fixed up. Alan is looking forward to having you stay there."

"Wonderful, Veronica. I can't thank you enough."

"It was a pleasure, my dear. And how was you romantic weekend at Bribie?"

"Marvellous. Just what the two of us needed. You know how grateful we always are for the use of your cottage. And to Helen for minding the boys all weekend, too. By the way," she continued, adjusting the piano stool as she spoke, "we had a little adventure in Andrew's boat."

"I'm all ears."

"Well, we took it out on the Sunday, quite early. Andrew had wanted us to give it a good run because he hasn't had it out on the water for a while. Anyway, we went right up the passage as far as Mission Point and went ashore to have our coffee and biscuits."

"And what else?" I muttered.

"Veronica, you have a disgusting mind! Anyway, just as we were packing up to get back in the boat, my hand felt something hard in the sand. I looked down, and found it was a small, gold necklace. It was... Oh damn! Here comes trouble!"

John Abbott had just walked in and was hurrying over to ask something.

"Yes, John. And what can we do for you?"

"Excuse me, Veronica. Miranda, I just wanted to check your part. There seems to be a misprint in your copy. It's in bar 38. Just before the..."

His words were drowned out by some of the brass warming up at the back of the stage. To save my ears, I got up and hurried over to ask Helen if she was going to the party after the concert. It was now twenty-five past seven and the stage was almost full. I was relieved to see that so far there was no sign of Sardor.

"Don't worry, Veronica," Miranda read my mind. "I think Mike scared him off last week."

"With his cheek, he'll probably just turn up to the concert after missing the final rehearsal."

"Can we have an 'A' please, Peter?" John's clear voice cut through the din. Peter, our principal oboe, was a retired detective from CIB. The orchestra was full of players with such interesting backgrounds. Doctors, dentists, lawyers and business people all happily shared music stands with the more expected music teachers and part time professional players. I was idly musing on this interesting social phenomenon when my concentration was sharply pulled back into focus by the sound of John's familiar, "Let's go!" End of gossip for the next ninety minutes. And although I was dying to find out more about this mysterious necklace buried in the sand, as luck would have it, Miranda and I got separated at coffee time. On top of this, Michael came early, doubtless feeling apprehensive about Sardor and anxious to whisk his newly restored beloved away to safety.

"I'll ring you later, Veronica," Miranda called over her shoulder as she hurried out the door.

Scene Six

Brisbane

I had been neglecting Sarah lately, so frantic was this time of the year. Like ships in the night, we passed each other with barely a ripple. To be sure, my sister was not at all the sort of person to sit around feeling sorry for herself. When Helen had married and left home, after a lot of soul searching from both of us, Sarah had sold the old family house up in Ipswich and moved in with me. It was a fantastic arrangement. While we greatly enjoyed each other's company, at the same time the long wisdom of our years had taught us both how to respect each other's privacy. And after the move, my fiercely independent sister had lost no time in joining the Brisbane branches of the organisations that had kept her so happy and occupied since her retirement as a matron at Ipswich Hospital. Bridge, meals on wheels, bushwalking, parish council and most recently, chess, all gave her ample stimulus and enjoyment. Life for us both was full and interesting.

Nevertheless, I felt it was high time now for some conversation a little more meaningful than "I think there's still some pasta left in the fridge", and "Would you be an angel and take out the rubbish bin this time?"

So it was that we found ourselves enjoying the rare treat of a slap-up lunch at the Kedron Brook Road café strip one fine November weekday just before the final concert of the Morelands Symphony.

"I hear our intrepid Miranda is going to Gympie again?" Sarah leaned back in her chair with a quizzical expression on her face.

"Yes. She has a couple of days' examining up there. Actually, I think the break will do her good, even though she wishes it was anywhere but Gympie."

"Why so?"

"Remember what happened to her up there that weekend?"

"Oh Lord, yes! How could I forget?"

"Well anyway, she'll feel much safer in Alan's flat than she would in a motel."

"Hmm! I wonder! And what if that idiot – Sardine or whatever he calls himself – comes after her?"

"He wouldn't know where she's staying. And after the bollocking Michael gave him I don't think he'd dare show his face. I did tell you, didn't I?"

"Indeed you did. *Arse over tit into the rose bushes.* I laughed till I cried. Wish I'd been there to see the fun."

We sat in silence for a minute. Sarah stirred her coffee thoughtfully, a frown on her face.

"What is it, old chum?"

"I've just had a dreadful thought."

I looked up, surprised. "What?"

"I know you'll say I'm panicking and I probably am. But didn't you and Helen find an old cutting in that chest of drawers you bought a while ago?"

"Well, yes. But what's so dreadful about an old news item?"

"I've been thinking about it for a while. For some reason, I can't get it out of my mind. And I can't remember the name of the criminal exactly, but wasn't it Sard something or other? Anyway I know he was a Hungarian, like this dude that's been annoying Miranda."

"Gosh, Sarah, your imagination's working overtime. Let me think … I remember now. No, it wasn't Sard anything. It was Szabo."

"Same thing," Sarah proclaimed with a delightful vagueness. "They're all much of a muchness in that Eastern Bloc. He's probably changed his name anyway."

"Maybe he did. But are you seriously suggesting that this Sardor is the same guy that pushed a student into the Salzach River all those years ago? And that having done that, he's somehow made his way halfway across the world and finished up here? Just so that he can do away with Miranda?"

"Stranger things have happened," she replied darkly.

"I daresay they have, and nothing's impossible. But Sarah, dear, just look at the probabilities. Okay, we know that Szabo escaped from Austria. We know that he was on the run, maybe still is. But how many countries in the world are there? What are the statistical chances of him turning up not only in Australia but in this very part of it? Anyway, he's probably dead as Julius Caesar by now."

"Well, I hope you're right, Veronica. You usually are. You're the level headed one."

"And you're the one with the gloomy Celtic imagination," I smiled, reaching for her hand. "Come on, Sis. We'd better go. Work calls."

"Furthermore," I added, *sotto voce,* as we paid our bill, "remember that even if he DID come after her, he wouldn't have a clue where she's staying. He'd go looking for her in some motel, now wouldn't he?"

"I suppose so. But I still have this really bad feeling. And I'm going to say some special prayers for her."

"Amen to that."

We got in the door just in time to catch the phone before it stopped ringing. It was none other than Miranda herself in her usual breathless rush.

"Veronica. Glad I caught you."

"We've only got back after a nice, leisurely lunch at Wilston."

"Some people! Anyway, in case things get too frantic at the concert tomorrow night, I just wanted to say a really big 'thank you' for all your trouble in arranging the flat at Gympie."

"A pleasure, my dear. And have you got all Alan's details? Phone numbers, address, etc?"

"Yep. All fixed up. I even rang him to introduce myself and he sounds a real sweetie."

"He certainly is. So's his wife Jane. By the way, Miranda, what about that necklace you and Michael found?"

"That was the other thing I rang about... Have you got a minute?"

"Sure."

"Well, it's obviously quite old. Like all lockets it's hinged, with an inscription meant to be on the inside part, but the whole thing had burst open. It looks as if it's been lying there like that for a very long time."

"How can you tell?"

"Because all the sand and gunk on it – which you'd expect – is caked on so hard it's like cement and it almost covers the inscription engraved in the centre."

"That's annoying."

"Isn't it? The little bit I can see says *To my* which really tells us a lot, doesn't it? Anyway, the locket itself is gold – could be just gilt since I'm no expert – but it's so pretty, Veronica. Heart shaped, and would you believe, after all the time it must have been there, the chain is still attached. Some of it's been broken off and it's shorter than it should be, but it's attached at one end. There are little stones all around the edge. Probably just rhinestones or maybe tiny diamond chips."

"Doesn't sound very valuable then. What are you going to do with it?"

"I think I'll clean it up and either wear it myself, if it looks okay, or else I might give it to Clare, or to one of Gemma's little girls."

"Wouldn't they just love that! Buried treasure! I think you'll have a fight on your hands."

Miranda laughed. "Well, I'll have to get all the muck off it first, won't I? Maybe tonight or even tomorrow morning. You know how much I love doing craftish things with my hands, and besides, it might help calm my nerves before the concert."

"Great idea. By the way, are you going to the party afterwards?"

"No, damn it! I'd love to, but I have this rotten early start first thing Sunday morning. After a late night and a performance, too, but it can't be helped. I'm due to begin examining at ten o'clock, with at least a two-hour drive beforehand."

"Bad luck, my dear. But I'm afraid that's just the luck of the game. The way the cookie crumbles."

"I know. Well, must dash, Veronica. And a million thanks again. I really couldn't have faced another motel, you know, with the constant thought of you know who coming after me. I know it's silly, but…"

"But it's entirely natural, sweetie. I'm sure I'd feel the same if I were in your shoes. However, you know that he's NOT going to come after you, and you also know that even if he did, he couldn't possibly know where you're staying. So if you can, just try to relax and enjoy the break. You'll be fine."

"I know I will, thanks to you. Well, I really must go this time. Until tomorrow night."

"Ciao."

ACT FIVE

Gympie. Late Sunday afternoon

I shall no more to sea, to sea,
Here will I die ashore

(*The Tempest*, Act One)

Scene One

Miranda drove into the yard and parked her car beside the decrepit old shed that had been a mattress room long ago in a previous incarnation when the shop had sold furniture and hardware. Now it reportedly housed spare lawnmowers, wheelbarrows, rakes and other assorted gardening equipment in its ancient, cavernous depths.

"I'm afraid the whole place looks rather tatty from the outside, Miranda," Alan had apologised. "That's one drawback when you have a rental property that's also being used as a business. No chance of even the most basic garden when you have trucks going in and out of the yard twenty times a day. Still, the tenants don't seem to mind because it's mostly rented out to singles or to working couples without any kids. And I think you'll find it very comfortable inside."

"I'm sure I will, Alan," Miranda replied gratefully. "I'm just so thankful that you and Jane were kind enough to let me use it for this couple of days."

"Well, it's no palace, I admit. But we've done our best to make it as homelike as possible and I guess if you value your privacy, it's a bit better than a motel. Anyway, here are the keys. You'll find it all set up for you. Milk, eggs, bacon, bread, butter and some fruit in the fridge and other basic supplies like tea and coffee. Make yourself at home, and don't forget to ring us if you have any concerns at all."

"Thanks a million, Alan," she smiled. "See you tomorrow evening, then."

Miranda was touched by the generosity of these kind people whom she hadn't even met until half an hour ago. Too exhausted to move now, she slumped back in her seat, re-living the taxing performance of the previous night, the too early start from home this morning, the long drive up the highway, followed by the full day of examining where every minute demands intense concentration. All of this had made her more fatigued than she had anticipated. Drifting off into a fitful doze, she was rudely jerked back into consciousness by the obscene "thump, thump, thump" of a car radio behind her as its idiot driver roared down Reef Street in a bright red Cortina on his way to an appointment with the morgue.

Better get out of this damned car before I crash for the night.

Wearily she picked up her handbag, dragging herself out of the driver's seat before collecting her overnight bag and examining satchel from the boot.

Well, Alan didn't lie when he said the place didn't look much from the outside, did he? Presumably the front of the shop which faced Mary Street was much more prepossessing. Here at the back entrance, the rough dirt yard led to an ugly wooden lean-to that had been tacked on to the main building some time over the years when more space was needed. The building itself appeared to be in good condition but the featureless brick walls were grimy and dark with age. Eight plain sash windows, four to each level, stared out sightlessly into the gathering darkness.

Securing her car carefully for the night, Miranda wended her way past the shed and up a short flight of external wooden stairs. Fitting her borrowed key into the door at the back of the building, she soon found herself standing inside a small vestibule dimly lit from the fading evening light which struggled to find its way through square window panes. Outside the window ominous clouds were forming, thick with the threat of storm. Ahead of her lay another door, securely locked, leading to the shop. A few feet to the right a steep, narrow flight of stairs disappeared into an unseen shadowy distance best not thought about. Fumbling for the light switch, she cautiously made her way upstairs. To her relief, another light at the top of the staircase revealed a large, pleasant hall, furnished with pot plants, comfortable chairs and a soft, brown leather couch.

The rest of the flat also lived up to Alan's modest claim that it was "homelike". Miranda wandered through the spacious rooms before finding the bedroom prepared for her, a pretty yellow room opening out on to the front veranda which overlooked the street. Throwing her bags on to the bed, she stepped out on to the narrow space edged with intricate, white painted iron lace and furnished with two sets of Colebrookdale tables and chairs. Below the veranda, Mary Street dipped and snaked its way down to a small valley where the five-ways occupied the lowest point of the town, only to have each road rise again sharply, with the whole landscape crowned by the stately Gothic style edifice of St Patrick's bestowing its blessing from the highest point beside Calton Hill. *What a pretty place. I wish I could stay a bit longer to enjoy it.* Sighing with renewed weariness, Miranda took off her uncomfortable work clothes and sprawled out on the bed in loose cotton pyjamas. *Just ten minutes of blissful nothingness before getting up to eat, check exam reports and shower before bed. That's all I need.*

*

It was the thunder that woke her. What time was it? It seemed hours later. With a start, Miranda sat up on the bed and looked out upon a world gone mad with elemental rage. Fierce gusts of wind hurled tattered paper scraps against the lamp posts and bent footpath trees almost double. Dark, indigo clouds behind the roof of the hotel over the road were pierced by forked lightning as deep torrents of water gushed down the black bitumen below, to the accompaniment of an incessant rain tattoo drumming on the iron roof of the veranda above.

Getting up hastily, Miranda made her way out to the hall at the top of the stairs. *That's funny. I'm sure I left that light on.* Cautiously she walked through the flat, anxiously trying every light. Not one of them worked. The stove clock, then? Or the microwave dial? Dead as Pompeii, both of them. Every switch in the flat equally defunct.

Just then, a savage gust of wind blew in an unwelcome shower of rain from the veranda. Remembering that when she had arrived, she had opened all the French doors because it was still so hot, she raced through the flat now, hastily snatching shut each door. The last thing this lovely old place needed was wet, ruined polished floors or worse still, smashed glass from the beautiful antique doors.

Lights. She must have lights or she'd go mad in this lonely, spectral gloom. Surely to heavens there must be matches and candles somewhere in this godforsaken place. Feeling her way blindly along the kitchen bench she managed at last to locate the pantry, meanwhile cursing herself for leaving her small emergency torch in the glove box of the car. She reached back gingerly past a bottle of what felt like instant coffee and a tin of Milo before finding at last the treasured box of matches. So far, so good. Now for the candles.

What was that? From far down below there came the faint sound of a door closing.

I'm imagining things. I know I locked that outer door. Shakily resuming her search for the elusive candles, she lit another match and peered still further into the back of the pantry.

A stair creaked. She froze. *It's a stout wooden door. Nobody can possibly get in.* Forcing herself to stay calm, she told herself that old buildings can often make strange sounds, especially at night. Her fingers still shook so badly that she could barely strike the next match.

A second stair creaked, louder this time, and nearer. Trembling violently as she swung round to face the gloomy hall, she heard the measured tread of feet on the staircase. A dark shape was inching its way along the far wall at the top of the steps. Then it came. The eerie, white lightning that flooded every corner of the room, painting the scene before her with its terrifying brilliance.

She looked into the smiling face of her attacker and stifled a scream as she swayed and clutched at a chair for support.

Scene Two

Brisbane – Saturday evening.

The concert had gone off very well. Oh, there were a few stuff-ups. There always are. Even professional orchestras don't escape the usual slips, lapses of concentration and other gremlins that are an inevitable part of any live performance. Such mishaps are usually so unobtrusive that even well-trained listeners can rarely detect them unless they happen to have an extremely detailed knowledge of the works played. Only in recordings, heavily edited, do you ever expect complete technical perfection – and yet, paradoxically, this very perfection is sometimes achieved at the expense of the real spontaneity and excitement of a live performance.

So it was that, glitches notwithstanding, we were all well pleased with our efforts tonight, and Helen and I congratulated ourselves as we travelled together to the after party to celebrate.

"There's nothing worse than getting all hyped up in a performance and then going straight home, is there?" she observed as we drove along the Western Freeway; "for me anyway. Besides, it's a chance to get to know the other players a bit better as you chew over the post mortems, I always think. "

"That's true. I'm certainly looking forward to it. I only hope that revolting Sardor doesn't show up."

"But Miranda isn't coming. She told me so tonight."

"I know. Just the same, I think I'd be tempted to knock his teeth out if I even had to look at him, after what he tried to do to her."

"Me too, Mum, but don't fuss. I know for certain he isn't coming because I saw him dash off straight after the concert and get into a taxi going in the other direction... Damn! I always get lost going to Jenny's place for cello tutorials. Don't talk to me until I'm off this stupid roundabout."

The stupid roundabout was negotiated in respectful silence without an unscheduled side trip to Sinnamon Park, so that we soon found ourselves at the front gate of a very attractive house on Mt Ommaney Drive, right on the river.

We went in through an open-plan tiled room, past the pool and out to a covered area looking out over the river.

"What a gorgeous spot!"

"Yes, isn't it? Hamish and I eat out here all the time except when the weather's bad. Oh come in, John. The man of the moment."

"Thanks to all you wonderful people. You did yourselves proud."

He spotted me and came over to give me a friendly pat on the shoulder. "Well done, Veronica. I'd hire you again any time."

"Not until I've had a decent break, thanks all the same, John. Sometimes I think I'm getting too old for this caper."

"Me too, but one must never give in, must one? Are you really going to have some time off now?"

"You bet. I'm going up to Bribie next week. Can't wait."

"Ah, Bribie, yes. Charming little place. I've been there a few times, but I'm afraid I..."

His words dissolved in a sea of general chatter as performers, sometimes accompanied with family members, continued to wander in at various intervals throughout the evening. Naturally I didn't know many of the players, since like Miranda, I was only a guest performer, yet for me the time still passed very pleasantly with good food, drink, and interesting company.

I glanced at my watch. Twenty to twelve.

"Jenny," John was saying to our hostess, his words a little slurred. "Jenny."

He reached out to hold her hand while she instinctively drew back a little.

"You remind me of my wife... No, not Marjorie. She's my second wife and David's my stepson... My first wife ... she was called Jenny too, you know."

"Did she ... did she leave you, John?"

"She died."

"I'm so sorry. What happened?"

"An accident. A boating accident. Out in the bay. Somewhere off Redcliffe. We were not long married. They never found her ... never found her. They looked and searched and then looked again. Water police, divers, the lot. Finally they gave up. The sharks probably got her."

I went and sat beside him. "Don't upset yourself, John. I lost my husband too."

"Then you'll know what it's like, won't you? Every day I think of her. Every single bloody day. Jenny. My sweet English rose, I used to call her. And now she's gone. She's gone and I'll never see her again." His eyes filled with tears which rolled unchecked down his cheeks.

There was nothing we could say. People started passing around what was left of dessert in the embarrassed silence that followed. I got up to stretch my legs and to get another lemon lime and bitters before the long drive home to McDowall.

"One for the road, eh Veronica?" I looked around to see Peter, the oboist, reaching into the Esky for a final beer.

"Reckon I might need this after that awful story. Did you know John had been married before?"

He propped, stubby poised in mid-air. "Well, as it happens, I did know, but most people up here don't because it all happened ages ago when he lived in Sydney and was up with his wife on holidays. And if he'd just eased up a bit on the grog tonight and kept his stupid trap shut no one in Brisbane would be any the wiser still."

"I don't understand, Peter. What's the problem? Why the deadly secrecy?"

He looked around. "You'd better come in here for a bit. This isn't for general consumption." I followed him into the empty kitchen, ears twitching.

"I guess I'll have to tell you now," he replied, *sotto voce*, "if only to forestall your perfectly innocent speculating to people less wise and less discreet than your good self. By the way, you're not a personal friend or anything, are you?"

"Heavens, no. I hardly know the man."

"That's good. Well, here goes. Did you know I used to work in CIB?"

"Yes I did. Helen told me."

"It all happened about forty years ago and I was just a young detective when Abbott's wife disappeared. I wasn't on the case myself and never met him, but we all knew about it in the department. And at the time, we weren't convinced that the disappearance was entirely innocent."

"What do you mean, Peter?"

"I mean that we suspected foul play."

"By *John?*"

"It's possible, but it probably wasn't by John himself. After all, he had no criminal record or history of violence whatsoever. One theory was that the tragedy could have been the result of some kind of brawl in a small, unstable boat with a third party on board. That unknown person would then have been up for manslaughter and John could well have been covering up for him – or her. You'd never know in a case like this one. Of course it could even have been an accident, as he always claimed at the time."

"But then why did they think it was suspicious in the first place?"

"Well, there were a few odd things about the whole business. For a start, his stated condition of the tides as against his times of departure and return just weren't correct for that day. He sold the boat in a mighty hurry before we could even begin more detailed investigations, then said he didn't keep a record of the buyer's identity because he was too distraught. We also noticed that he seemed quite evasive when asked to describe exactly how the accident actually occurred. Changed his story substantially several times. And to cap it all, no trace of the body was ever recovered."

"Sharks?"

"Quite possibly. There could be a hundred and one reasons for not finding a body especially in a maritime fatality. But still…"

"But still, you weren't sure?"

"No, we weren't. You know, Veronica, in our game, you try to forget most crimes or suspected crimes that you deal with over the years. That's how you cope. You'd go crazy otherwise. Nevertheless there are always a few that stick in your mind, even cold cases like this one. I suppose it's because I hate unsolved mysteries."

"So do I, but only in books. Helen says I'm addicted to crime."

"Just on paper, I hope. I don't have my handcuffs any more," he laughed.

"No, Peter, you can relax. I only like crime that isn't real, thank God… But gosh! What a story! And I don't suppose there's anything you can do about it now, is there?"

"Not a darned thing. But do remember, Veronica, that I am able to tell you all this only because the whole thing was just a suspicion, not even an unproven fact. When this happens, we can't tell anyone. And remember, too, that the man is entitled to his good reputation in this city and that it MAY have been an accident all along."

"Then I suppose we'll never know."

"Never know what?" Helen appeared in the doorway. "Oh there you are, Mum. I've been looking for you. Isn't she awful, Peter? Flirting at her age… Are you ready to go now, Jezebel?"

"Yes, Mother Superior. Time we all called it a night. Let's just go and say goodnight to Jenny and to John if he's still there."

John was there all right, lounging back in a cane chair, pleasantly tipsy and holding forth to an increasingly bored and restless audience who were more than ready for bed. People surreptitiously started to leave.

"You know, it's actually NOT Béla Bartók at all. That's what all the peasants say. Anyone who knows anything about

Hungarians would know that they reverse their names. And anyway, the correct pronunciation sounds something like Bairtosch Beela...Your fact for the night, ladies and gentlemen," he added with a flourish.

Unaware of anything beyond the sheer joy of airing his exquisite, superior knowledge, he beamed indulgently at his rapidly disappearing audience, at which point we too, made a strategic exit.

Scene Three

Brisbane

I had a terrible night. Normally I sleep very well for my age, with only a few side trips to the bathroom which I have trained myself to make in the dark while maintaining a state of near unconsciousness. Likewise Sarah, who sleeps like a log and sounds like an army of timber cutters with chainsaws when she snores.

This night was different. Perhaps it was the elevated adrenalin that usually goes with most performances. Perhaps it was the unaccustomed stimulus of the after party and the resulting late bedtime. More likely, it was the disturbing story about John Abbott that Peter had told me. Try as I might, I couldn't get it out of my mind. Meanwhile I thrashed around, changed position a thousand times, twitched, turned over yet again, and heard every half hour strike on the grandfather clock in the hall until three o'clock.

I gave up in disgust then, and making sure that I didn't wake my sister from her happy timber cutting, padded out to the kitchen for a mug of hot milk. This time-honoured remedy usually does the trick for me, or if really desperate, I have a quick shower even though I've already had one before bed. Somehow the soothing hot water always seems to relax tense muscles.

Not this time. Alright then. Where's that book? Quietly, I tip-toed past Sarah's bedroom and into the living room where I knew I had left my latest P.D. James mystery. I could happily revel in fictional crimes, but a real one? No, thank you. Abbott and his questionable past were well outside my sphere and I intended to leave them right there. Having settled this, I was on my way back to bed, book in hand and desperately praying that I'd pass out after the second page.

Oh God! No! Can't be! I froze in my tracks just outside the kitchen door, as I remembered it. The name of Miranda's co-examiner for the Diploma session in Gympie the next afternoon.

John Abbott.

Now sick with fear, I sat down at the kitchen table, head in hands. This sweet, defenceless girl would certainly be safe working alone during the morning session examining the lower grades, but if Peter was right, all afternoon she would be working at close quarters with a possible killer. So trivial a detail was the identity of her colleague for the advanced examinations that I had remembered it only this very instant.

Now ... calm down, Veronica. Abbott only *might* be a killer. And even if he DID kill his wife, wasn't that many, many years ago? People do change, you know. Furthermore, what possible motive could he have for harming Miranda? And why would he want to risk his good reputation here, especially now that's he's happily retired?

I don't know. But I feel uneasy. No wonder I haven't been able to sleep.

"I still have this really bad feeling."

Sarah's words at the coffee shop that day only last week

But wasn't she was talking about Sardor then?

Forget Abbott. He's harmless.

The whole thing's ridiculous. I'm going back to bed.

This time I did manage to get to sleep. Worn out by the performance, the party and the hours of tedious wakefulness, I fell at last into a deep torpor which lasted until I heard the clock strike six. I'm not getting up yet. Much too early. Rolling over, I thankfully went back to sleep straight away, but this time there was to be no pleasant nothingness. The next three hours were punctuated by hideous dreams that twisted and turned and melded one into the other in a kaleidoscope of shifting horrors.

    First of all, the leering face of Frank Sardor pushed itself so close to me that I felt I couldn't breathe.
    "Get out! Get out!" I cried angrily, swatting at him with hands that suddenly went limp and had no power. He puckered up his blubbery lips for a kiss and then smirked obsequiously before retreating slowly and morphing into a boat which contained old Seth holding his fishing line with his dog panting beside him in the prow.
    "I tell you this, lady. There's more things in Davy Jones' locker than you could poke a stick at." Last of all came the figure of John Abbott, baton in hand, bowing endlessly to left and right before an adoring audience. "I'm so pleased you could play for us, Veronica," he turned and smiled at me, "but now I have some unfinished business to attend to."

*

"Veronica ... Veronica. Are you alright?" Sarah was knocking anxiously on my door, a cup of tea in her hand.
    "Come in, come in. Yes, I'm okay. Why?"
    "It's after nine o'clock." She sat down on the bed.
    "Can't be... Ye gods, so it is ... sorry, but we'll have to go to a later Mass."
    "Don't worry about that. We can still catch the ten o'clock at St Brigid's. Anyway, what's wrong? You never sleep this late."
    "I know. But I had a pretty rugged night. I didn't sleep at all until well after three o'clock."
    "Were you hyped up after the concert or something?"
    "Bit more than that. Give us a sec and I'll come out and tell you."
    Over a rushed breakfast, I filled Sarah in on the essentials of what Peter had told me at the party. I had persuaded myself that Abbott was no threat to Miranda, but last night's feeling of unease

returned this morning with a vengeance. And much as I had wanted to keep it all to myself, as promised, I realised that this was impossible for me now. Miranda may be involved, however indirectly, and if there was even a remote threat to her safety, I had to do something about it. I would keep my promise not to broadcast it, but I would have to tell Sarah everything. She would know anyway that I had something serious on my mind. And while I knew she could be impulsive and sometimes tactless in small things, I knew also that where it really counted, she was the very soul of discretion. I could rely on her one hundred percent.

*

After church and a late lunch, I tried valiantly to relax, but it was no good. Unlike my highly strung daughter, I'm normally a fairly tranquil person. However, all afternoon I was consumed by an uncharacteristic restlessness coupled with a sharp sense of urgency. I knew I had to do something without having the faintest idea what it was.

"Veronica, you've been pacing around this house like a caged lion," Sarah scolded. "I can't stand it another minute. Here. Sit down. Take this pad and pen. Write down everything you can think of that's bothering you. It will help clear your head."

"Yes, Matron! No Matron! I obey, Matron."

"Don't be an idiot." She clouted me affectionately behind the ear. "Now be a good girl and do your homework. I'll be playing Patience in the living room if you need a second brain."

Okay. Here we go. Where do I start?
John Abbott. Could have killed first wife.
Where?
Moreton Bay. Somewhere off Redcliffe.
Body never recovered, so could be lying about the "where". If I killed someone, wouldn't I give a different location to save my skin?

Maybe. But it would have to be in the vicinity. Otherwise too difficult to lie convincingly.

I dreamt last night about old Seth. Is my subconscious trying to tell me something?

Okay. Let's leave John for a minute.

Davy Jones' locker.

The mysterious boat which got stuck on the sandbank and the man in that boat who refused help. "Two went up and one come back."

I remembered his words so clearly because it was only a couple of weeks ago.

Let's look at the other parts of the dream.

John Abbott has some unfinished business.

If he really did kill his first wife, you bet he has some unfinished business. Like a whole lifetime of the most massive guilt.

Stop relying on dreams, you dumbo. Stick to facts.

Okay. Facts for now

Fact. Seth witnessed a mysterious disappearance at sea forty years ago.

Fact. Abbott's wife disappeared in the same region. Forty years ago, more or less.

Fact. The police had their suspicions at the time.

Fact. Abbott kept changing his story

Fact. Abbott sold his boat in a hurry.

Fact. Miranda was assaulted by Sardor.

Fact. He may still be a threat, even though I tried to reassure her.

Fact. Sardor is Hungarian. Sarah has this wild idea he could be the escaped Szabo. I don't believe it for a minute. But let's put it into the frame, just in case.

You dreamed about Sardor, didn't you?

Yes, but. We're doing facts right now, aren't we?

Known facts all accounted for. Now for some theories.
If Abbott killed his wife, then why?
Money? Not likely. Abbot isn't rich.
Another woman? Could be. Is Marjorie that woman? But wouldn't divorce have been a lot easier than murder?
Did wife number one know something?
More likely. But if so, then what?
If there WAS a third person in the boat, could it have been Sardor? And did Abbott and Sardor have some previous connection? Don't know.

By now my head was spinning so much with these multiple possibilities that I was more than glad to see Sarah standing in the doorway, a thoughtful expression on her face.

"Veronica," she asked, "I know this probably hasn't got anything to do with anything but I've suddenly had a hunch. Did Miranda ever find out anything more about that necklace she found up at Bribie last week?"

"Not sure, but I do know that she was hoping to clean it up the night before the concert. Why?"

"I thought you said it had some kind of an inscription on it."

"That's right. She said it had, but that she could only make out the first two words on it. Do you think it might be important?"

"Dunno. Could be. Like I said, it's just a hunch. Probably doesn't mean anything."

"Perhaps not, but it wouldn't hurt to find out anyway. You see, I've been remembering the story that old Seth told me about the mysterious boat going up the passage with two people and coming back with only one."

"And where exactly did Miranda find the necklace?"

"At Mission Point, she said."

"Well, that's certainly in the wrong direction for anyone getting drowned near Redcliffe. But it could square with what Seth told you about that other boat. Couldn't it?"

"Indeed it could, dear heart. You know, Sarah, we're probably looking at two entirely separate mysteries, or even at one mystery and one perfectly innocent accident at sea. Just the same, I think

I'll ring Michael now. At the very least, I'm fascinated by the idea of a necklace buried in sand for so many years. And there's just a chance that Miranda may have cleaned the gunk off the inscription. She's probably left the necklace behind her at home this weekend and hopefully, Michael can find it."

Michael couldn't find it. Miranda had taken it with her to Gympie.

"I'm sorry, but it's not here, Veronica. She put it in her handbag to show you at the concert, then forgot all about it. And she was in such a rush getting ready for the trip after the late night that she took off with it. When she rang me from Gympie this morning she was joking about my not being able to wear the darned thing with my new shirt. Said she'd give it to Clare when she got back."

"Oh!"

"Why, is something wrong? It's not a valuable piece of jewellery, you know. Only an old lost trinket."

"I know, Mike. It's just that I was interested to know what the inscription said. I love old furniture, old jewellery. Anything with a history. It's only a hobby."

"Well in that case I can satisfy your curiosity. It was such hard work cleaning off all those years of accumulated dirt which had practically turned to cement that I helped Miranda do it. We finished it on Saturday afternoon."

"Can you remember what it said?"

"I certainly can, since it was such a slow job that we both had ample time to observe it."

"You're an angel, Michael."

*

"Well," demanded Sarah, "what news?"

"Ssh!" I replied, "I'm trying to remember something and I can't think what."

"Take your time. It will come to you."

The party. Something about the party. The evening had passed in a pleasant whirl and the only thing that had really stuck in my mind was Peter's astounding revelation about John Abbott. Think, Veronica. Think. Before Peter. Someone said something but you only half took it in because everyone was so embarrassed when John broke down about his first wife. I do remember he said something about never seeing her again, but I'm certain there was something else. Come on, come on. What was it? Dear Lord, please help me remember.

Sarah waited patiently. "Any luck?"

"YES! Yes! I think I've got it! ... I'm sure he said *Every day I think about her. Every single bloody day. Jenny. My sweet English rose, I used to call her.*"

"And what is on the inscription, Veronica? ... Please don't look like that, sweetheart. You've gone as white as a sheet."

"It says, *To my sweet English rose, Genevieve. All my love. Franky.*

*

Sarah got up swiftly to make me a cup of hot, strong tea.

"Here, drink this. You look like death."

"Thanks," my hands were shaking as I held the mug.

We sat in silence for a full minute, trying to digest the terrifying implications of this innocent inscription.

"Who's Franky? Not that appalling Frank Sardor?"

I thought for a minute.

"No... No, it can't be. Andrew promised he'd keep digging about Sardor's past, and he found out only the other day that the first wife was Hungarian and the second one Australian. The owner of the necklace was English. But the inscription seems to fit Abbott's wife. Jenny is a common abbreviation of Genevieve and he used to call her his "sweet English rose" all of which is the exact dedication on the locket. Furthermore, his first wife was lost at least somewhere in this area. And the police always had their suspicions. It's all just too much of a coincidence. But Franky? I can't work that part out."

Sarah frowned in concentration. "You know how people sometimes get called by their second name? Like our mum. Couldn't he have been christened Frank John Abbott?"

"Yes. Yes he could," I replied slowly, "except ... except that one night at rehearsal I saw his briefcase on the stage when I was helping put music stands away. And I'm certain the gold initials on the leather were J H Abbott. No sign of an F anywhere. I'm sure of it."

"Well, I'd trust your powers of observation, any time, Veronica. Miss Eagle-eye, I used to call you when you were little."

"Comes in handy sometimes, doesn't it?" I managed a smile. "Anyway, I'm buggered thinking about all this. I think my head's going to explode. Let's have a quick dinner and rest our tired brains for half an hour."

*

"Why would he put his first name on the locket when he never used it later?" Sarah asked through a mouthful of spag bol.

"Don't know. Maybe he hated it and just used it used it with her as a pet name for a joke, or something. Like you used to call me Twinky. You know, it also reminds me of the story about CS Lewis, the writer. Apparently he didn't like Clive, the name he was given. So one day when he was only four years old he suddenly pointed to his chest and announced to the world, '**He ... He** is Jacksie' and Jack he remained for the rest of his life."

"Well, I'd probably do the same thing too, if I'd been landed with a clunker like Clive Staples Lewis. But why Frank? It's not such a bad name, is it?"

"No it's not. I mean ... if it was something outlandish like ... oh, like Friedrich, or Ferdinand or Frankenstein or even Franz you might want to ditch it. And we've had to rule out our dear friend Frank Frog's Eyes."

"You're getting awfully European."

"Yes, aren't I? Oh I give up. It's getting way too hard."

"Giving up on Miranda?" Sarah's blue eyes held a hint of disapproval.

"Well, no. I didn't mean that. Oh Sarah, I really don't know what I mean. I'm so tired I can't think straight."

"Then let me help you. As you said before, we probably have two entirely separate puzzles. One, let's suppose for the moment that the necklace did belong to Abbott's first wife. As you said, it seems too much of a coincidence otherwise, despite the donor's wrong name. By the way, I take it that Abbott would never have let his guard down like that at the party if he hadn't been a bit tipsy."

"No, he wouldn't. He's always played his cards close to his chest."

"Right. So we've *probably* got the answer to puzzle one. The owner of the necklace. Puzzle two. Franky. If we're right, then it must have been his name at some point. I mean, it's not a silly nickname like 'Twinky', is it? So it must have been his actual name before he changed it. Changed his whole name, I mean."

"You're joking, Sarah. In heaven's name, why?"

"Because, my dear, he's changed his whole identity."

"*What?*"

"People do, you know. All the time. I've seen it happen with patients at the hospital. And sometimes the reason is quite innocent, too."

"But not this time?"

"No. Not this time. I'd stake my life on it."

This was getting worse than an Agatha Christie mystery. How badly we needed Poirot's little grey cells.

"Then why?"

"Because he had to."

"Whatever for? To cover up something?"

"Well, why else? He's English, so he's obviously not changing identity because of something like political persecution or personal danger. England is a safe country and a stable democracy. Which leaves just one reason. He's on the run."

"From what?"

Sarah got up to stretch her legs. I followed her into the kitchen.
"From something he did before he became John Abbott."
"And?"
"And we suspect he killed his first wife. Why? Money? No. Other woman? Unlikely. Which to my mind at least means that the wife probably found out something she shouldn't."
"Like what?"
I leaned over the sink, utterly exhausted. My sister came over and put an arm around my shoulders, swinging me round to face her.
"Like this. I know we've had this conversation before. And you've often teased me about my wild Celtic imagination. Remember how you joked about it that time we talked about the escaped Szabo and I thought it was Sardor? Well, try this one on for size. *Abbott, not Sardor, is Szabo.*"
"You're out of your mind."
"I know, I know. It's highly improbable. Or it would be, except for this one thing that we've both been forgetting. Think back to that newspaper cutting."
I racked my brains.
"Szabo," Sarah prompted. "What was his full name?"
"Ferenc ... Johannes ... Szabo," I said slowly.
"That's right. **Johannes ... John.**"
"Oh good grief, Sarah, our missing link. But it's a long shot."
"Yes, I know it is. And I know I've been fixated on the escaped Hungarian murderer, and I'm letting my intuition run riot, but think, Veronica. Think. Is there anything at all about John Abbott that strikes you as being non British? Any small quirk that you may have noticed, even unconsciously? It's a million to one chance, but we have to exclude the possibility, or at least try to, for Miranda's sake. It wouldn't be so urgent except for that blasted necklace she's got with her. They're working at close quarters all afternoon, sharing a desk. What if he somehow finds out that she's got the damn thing? It doesn't bear thinking about, does it?"

I racked my brains. Nothing came, nothing at all.

Then in a flash it appeared quite unbidden – a memory of those last five minutes at the party last night. Abbott, half-drunk, lounging back in his chair, holding forth about Bartók. It had all seemed so unimportant at the time that it had barely registered.

You know, it's actually not Béla Bartók at all. Anyone who knows anything about Hungarians would know that they reverse their names. And anyway, the correct pronunciation sounds something like Bairtosch Beela.

How had I missed it? How stupid could I have been? That curious, non-English pronunciation that only a native born Hungarian could ever produce so accurately? With my sharp ear for both music and words, why had I been so slow to notice those other strange little inflections hidden cleverly in that refined BBC accent? My brain was flooded now with an avalanche of impressions that I had never been consciously aware of over the last few weeks. The telltale, expressive hand gestures so natural to Europeans but so foreign to the buttoned-up British. The unusually sensitive empathy with Hungarian music. The physical appearance, even. The greying, dark hair, the brown eyes, the high Slavic cheekbones common in many Hungarians but very rare in native born Englishmen. Each detail a tiny brush stroke, insignificant when viewed alone, but aligning themselves together on the canvas of the mind to paint a sickening picture of corruption and evil.

The name.

How do you change it?

What would you do?

Start with the name you have? Very likely. But if so, then you would have to alter it into something that sounds so quintessentially English that it would fool even the Queen.

Okay. Let's try it.

Ferenc Johannes Szabo.

Frank John Szabo … Sabo … Abo … Abot … Abbott.

Frank John Abbott.

Nearly. But not quite

Frank must go. Any official agency trying to trace you can easily recognise Frank as the anglicised form of Ferenc. But a common name like John? What could be safer?

Let it be John, then. But you're not there yet. You're still very young. Deception is still a developing art, and the unhealed wounds of personality mutilation are so raw and painful that in your mind you remain the Ferenc of your recent boyhood. You even shared that name with Liszt, your famous countryman. So for a while you use the English version as a nickname in the privacy of your home with your innocent young wife. She sometimes teases you by calling you Franky. But never, never in public. Haven't you ensured her discretion by telling her that it's your own precious secret to be kept for just the two of you? She loves you so she humours you. She knows nothing about your real background; she will never suspect you, not until the very end. But when she's disposed of, then for God's sake get rid of the bloody thing. In this final, brutal surrender, you succeed in destroying not only your very identity but your precious, God-given soul.

The massacre is complete. Ferenc Szabo is dead. Genevieve is dead. You are now Mr John Henry Abbott from Beckenham, educated at the Royal College and as English as a pork pie.

The last pieces of the kaleidoscope had fallen into place. I sat back, weak with shock.

*

"Police? Emergency services?" Sarah, quick on the uptake, as always.

I shook my head. "They won't act on a mere supposition. It's only a theory even if you and I believe it's absolutely true. No, I have a better idea."

I raced over to the phone, "Alan, it's Veronica here. Sorry there's no time to explain now, but would you please go round to the flat immediately and check up on Miranda? And take a couple of able-bodied blokes with you. There may be someone else with her who could be dangerous. Police, no. Not yet. I'll tell you why later."

"You know," observed Sarah, relaxing for the first time in hours, "I'm the one backtracking now. We could be panicking for nothing. There's no certainty that Abbott will ever suspect she has the necklace."

"No, but what if he does? Miranda's such a chatty girl she could easily have told him all about it or it could even have fallen on to the desk out of her handbag when she was rummaging for a biro to start her examining session. I've often had things fall out of my bag just like that."

"Then we can't afford to take a risk, can we? And are you going to ring Michael?"

"Yes. Right now."

Scene Four

Gympie

It was Sardor all over again. A repeat performance. Same act, but different scene, different cast...

"What do you want? I locked that door. You scared the shit out of me bursting in like this. Why didn't you knock?"

"Couldn't make you hear."

Miranda shrank back against the wall. He read her body language with experienced eyes. "Relax, my dear. I haven't come to rape you."

"Then what HAVE you come for? I'm damn sure you haven't broken into this flat in the middle of a raging storm just to get those Diploma reports. Anyway, I know I gave them to you."

"So you did, my dear. So you did." Abbott laughed disparagingly, a sound so vile that it turned her stomach. "You're a funny girl. Always were. So naïve. So trusting. So literal minded. So like the narrow little suburban piano teacher that you are. You're all provincial hicks, you Queenslanders."

"Shut up, John. I'm not listening to this crap. Just get to the point."

"All in good time, sweetheart. You and I need to have a little chat first."

"About what?"

"About something you're going to give me."

"You're mad. I haven't got anything to give you."

"Oh yes you have, and no, I'm not the one that's mad. Never been saner in fact," he replied smoothly, advancing a step towards her. She retreated further, away from the hall and back into the kitchen.

"Relax, my love, just relax. I'm not going to hurt you. It's very simple. Just get me that necklace and it will all be over soon."

"WHAT necklace? I don't own an atom of valuable jewellery except my engagement ring and you're not getting that."

"The necklace that fell out of your bag today. I want it."

"What on earth for?" *He IS mad to want a cheap little trinket like that. He must have some warped fixation on women's jewellery; I've heard of sickos like that; he's dangerous.* Her initial shock and puzzlement gave way to pure terror. *I have to stall him. I need to play for time.*

Too late. In a rapid movement, he grabbed her arm and held it behind her back in an agonising twist. Remembering her self-defence lessons, she reacted with a swift backward kick but he was quicker. Both arms were pinned behind her back in a vice-like grip.

"Now march, young lady. I SAID MARCH. Into the bedroom or wherever it is you keep your handbag."

The bedroom. That's a piece of luck. If I can get out on to the veranda, I can scream for help, though I'll be flat out being heard in this bloody storm.

Stay calm, Miranda. Humour him. It's your best chance.

"And why do you want this necklace, John? It's not valuable."

"Why do I want it? You stupid little bitch, I want it because without it, I'm a dead man, or as good as dead. Caged behind bars like an animal for the rest of my life."

"You're talking rubbish."

"Am I? Then just you tell me what that inscription on the necklace says. Go on. Repeat it."

"To my sweet English rose, Genevieve. All my love, Fr…" She choked on the rest of her words as his tie went around her neck.

"That's right. Clever girl. You'll get a sticker for good work … KEEP STILL, DAMN YOU… You asked me why I want it, and now you're going to hear it whether you want to or not. You won't be around much longer to tell anyone else so you're no threat. Genevieve was my wife. My beautiful wife that I killed near Mission Point. I loved her. God I loved her. But she got in my way. She found out about my little encounter with Heinrich Schwartzkopf back in Salzburg. Found out that I was born in Budapest, not Beckenham. Found out that I was a killer. She got in my way, so she had to go. Just like you have to go."

At once, an incongruous schoolyard scene flashed into Miranda's mind. She remembered how her boys and their mates would sometimes link arms at lunchtime and march through the grounds, advancing with mock menace on the little grade one kids and chanting, "Anybody in the road gets runned over."

Patrick. Fabian. My precious little boys. Michael, my lost love, so newly returned. I'm never going to see them again. Sudden tears welled up in her eyes, but so tight was the pressure on her throat that she couldn't even cry. *Just get this over with, you bastard. I can't stand any more of this.*

"Nearly there, my dear. I've told you quite enough to satisfy your curiosity. It'll be all over soon. Then I'll drag you down the stairs, put you in the boot of my car and drive out to the river. They won't find you for days. I know what Michael did. *Oh poor Miranda. She was so depressed when her husband played up. Suicide of course. Isn't it awful?*

She barely heard those last words, so deeply was she drowning in a sea of unconsciousness. Neither did she hear nor see the veranda chair that became suddenly airborne in the fierce gust of wind that sent it smashing through the glass door and shattered the pane into myriad shards of destruction, with two huge spears finding their targets.

*

"Get a towel. Something. Anything. She's losing a lot of blood from that ankle."

"The ambulance is on its way."

"Thank God. What about him?"
Alan felt for a pulse.
He shook his head.
"Too late. He got it in the neck. He's gone."

Scene Five

Bribie Island

"How's Miranda?"
    "A mess, as you'd expect."
    "I hear Sardor has left the orchestra."
    "Yes, and good riddance."

    Christmas holidays. Helen and I were sitting at a picnic table in one of our favourite spots on the island. Buckley's Hole. Ahead of us, squads of ducks paddled their placid way like cross river ferries back and forth from the banks to the rough clumps of grass in the middle of the lake. A black swan dipped its head under the water before insolently shaking off the drops and continuing its stately procession across the surface. Clearly, this swan ruled the world.
    Helen gave a sigh and changed position on the hard wooden seat.
    "It's a bit of *déjà vu*, don't you think, Mum?" Her eyes filled with tears. "Two of us from the same set of friends looking death in the face."
    "And two of you staring it down," I replied quickly. "Darling, your experience and Miranda's were hideous beyond belief. But you survived."
    "Just."
    "Yes, as you say. Just. We all know the hell you went through for years afterwards. And we who love you could only stand by helplessly and watch, ready to give whatever comfort we could.

But in the end, you did come through it. Better, wiser, stronger and more compassionate than you ever were before."

"I guess so."

"Come on, possum." I gathered up the scraps from our picnic lunch. "Miranda's a fighter. Like you. It will take time, years maybe, but she'll make it in the end. As you did."

EPILOGUE

They found her under a pine tree, buried in a shallow grave covered with Nature's gentle blanket forty years in the making.

"We should send her home," Sergeant Tyler said, wiping the midday sweat from his forehead. The heat was stifling and mosquitos buzzed like a chorus of demented bees.

"Were they married in England?" Constable Barrett asked, leaning on his shovel.

"So I've been told. We've been able to get some records from his widow and from the Sydney Conservatorium where Abbott spent most of his working life before retiring to Queensland."

"Then it should be relatively easy to locate a marriage certificate in the UK, shouldn't it?"

"We're on to it already," Tyler answered. "Come on, Jim. Better start packing up. Seems like hours since I rang the location through to SOC and Forensics. What the hell are they doing?"

"Hang on. I think they're coming now. Yes, they are. I can see the boat. Looks like they've just left Donnybrook."

"Thank God. Between the heat and the mozzies, I'll be a basket case if I stay here much longer."

*

He came out on the first available flight a few weeks later. Her brother, Harry Yates, finally traced to an address at Hythe in Kent. All his life he had been haunted by the vision of a little girl falling helplessly into a canal in their backyard at Dymchurch.

Other memories, precious and painful, came flooding back on the long journey to Brisbane. Genevieve, dripping wet and covered with water weeds, crying and stamping her little feet.

"I'm never going near water again. I HATE you, Harry Yates."

Genevieve as a teenager, smiling up at him as she played with her dogs on the lawn. Genevieve with her new husband on the wharf at Tilbury docks, fighting back tears among all the excitement. "Don't be so glum, you silly old goose. We'll see each other again lots of times. You'll visit us in Australia and I'll come home whenever I can."

She came home, a lifetime later. He decked her coffin with her favourite daffodils and buried her in a churchyard beneath ancient yew trees, not far from the house he had shared for many happy years with his wife and children.

Rest in peace, sweet Genevieve.

*

Printed in Australia
AUOC010852170412
251943AU00001B/1/P